Rise of Dragons – Book 2

Solstice of Dragons

G Clatworthy

Find more at www.gemmaclatworthy.com

Cover art by Sanjay Charlon, Beehive Illustrations.

Foreword

Thank you to the amazing first readers, terrific typo hunters and grammar gurus – you are awesome!

This series is for my D&D group whose stories always inspire me!

Please join the conversation at Gemma's book wyrms or find Gemma on Instagram (www.instagram.com/gemmaclatworthy) or Facebook (www.facebook.com/gemmaclatworthy).

Chapter 1

I woke up suddenly, instantly alert. My senses were heightened. My room was dark. Living above my shop in Royal Arcade protected me from the ever present orange glow of the lamp posts that pervaded Cardiff homes on normal streets. Errol was growling softly at the end of the bed. His short wings were tucked up and his claws dug painfully into my leg underneath the thin sheets. I winced but stayed still. It was unlike the small wyrm to get spooked over nothing. Without moving my head, I looked around the room and listened carefully.

Was it my imagination or did I hear a rustle of fabric? Was there a shape in my small flat?

I ran through the options in my head. I could scream but I was the only one who lived in the Arcade. The owner had allowed me to stay in exchange for taking on the unit which had a draughty chimney built into the back room. Perfect for the small forge I had created for my jewellery and more illicit weapons business, but discouraging to other tenants. It was doubtful even my hearty lungs could shout loud enough to attract attention from the street and it wasn't like the Arcade was particularly close to any all-night bars. Plus I wasn't really a screaming kind of girl.

There was Bane, my trusty double headed ancestral axe stashed under my bed. Ever since my experience with the Awakener cult earlier in the year, I had felt safer with it near me at all times. Now it seemed too far away to reach easily.

I opted for turning my bedside lamp on with a yawn and a stretch as if I had just awoken naturally and was going to the toilet in the middle of the night. What a moron. I was acting for a potential burglar. Errol was still growling as he jumped off the bed and stood next to me, radiating heat and allowing small curls of smoke to escape from his nostrils.

I looked around. Nothing. No strange deep shadows in the corner. No stranger standing over my bed with a pointed dagger. I thought I heard a scuff downstairs in my shop. Of course! If anyone was in here they would be trying to rob the jewellery store not my postage stamp of a flat. I cautiously shifted my legs and stood on the hardwood floor as softly as I could. I bent over and slipped Bane from under the bed, holding my breath as it dragged over the floor. Then I padded lightly to the open staircase that led down to my shop.

"Hello?" I said nervously. What a moron. I rolled my eyes at myself and then ran down the stairs, holding my axe high and trying to look menacing. I caught my reflection in the mirrored glass as I sprinted into the middle of the shop. My oversized superhero t-shirt, sharp axe and wildly dishevelled hair made me look like a crazy person. I blinked then turned threateningly. Even better! Maybe whoever was here would run away at the sight of my pale legs and wild hair.

No one was there. I flicked on the lights, gripping Bane tightly, expecting someone to jump at me. Nothing. With more confidence, I checked behind the shabby chic counter. Nothing.

Then I heard a strange scrabbling sound from the back room behind the counter where I kept my forge and my under-the-counter weapons.

With a deep breath, I kicked back the door to my small forge. No one ran out. I turned the light on. Errol was sat next to his coal bucket, chewing on a large piece of finest Welsh coal. He looked at me and gave a dragony grin.

"If you woke me up just so you could get a midnight snack…" I started, waving my axe towards him. I let out a huff of annoyance as I flipped the lights off and prepared to go back to bed. Something caught my eye as I walked back through the shop. I peered over at the door then checked it. Locked. Shrugging, I heaved Bane onto my shoulder and whistled a little too loudly as I got back into bed and snuggled under the covers.

I shoved Bane under my pillow then shifted uncomfortably. In films when the hero keeps a weapon under their pillow, it seems sensible and cool. Easy to reach, good for defending yourself. Maybe there's a reason it's never an axe because having a large axe in bed with me was not comfortable. Even with the thickness of a pillow between me and it, the axe was hard and dug into my head. After trying a few different positions, I sighed and rested it against my bedside table. At least I could reach it easily.

Errol scrabbled back upstairs after finishing his midnight snack and curled up, his body a small hot water bottle against my stomach. I lay on the bed, staring at the ceiling. I still felt uneasy so left my lamp on, the wizard lampshade casting strange shadows around the room. The strange brown stain on the ceiling mocked me as I stared up at it. There's nothing there, I told myself, but I couldn't shake the sensation that someone had been in my shop and I didn't feel quite as safe in my flat as I usually did.

I must have dropped off eventually because my alarm woke me, blaring in my ear, dragging me from slumber. Schiztz, why was it so loud? I tapped my phone to turn it off and realised it wasn't my alarm, it was my parents calling.

Blearily I answered, "Hello Mum."

"Hi darling, I didn't wake you did I?" Mum's voice sounded bright and cheery.

I held the phone away from my face and blinked at the display. 6:05 am. Who calls just after six in the morning?

"I just didn't sleep well last night, that's all."

"Well I'll get right to it then you can go back to bed." Mum carried on breezily, "Your Dad and I are coming into town so I wanted to make sure you were free for dinner," I stared at my gothic wizard lamp and frowned. Mum sensed my hesitation, "You didn't forget we were coming did you? I'm sure I told you if you didn't visit, we were coming to see you…and we haven't seen you in such a long time."

I scratched Errol behind the ears and he grumbled lazily, he didn't like being woken up either.

"Erm, well I don't remember you saying you were coming today. I'm really busy gaming with Aloora…" I tried.

Mum laughed giddily. "Not tonight silly." I breathed a sigh of relief. Mum pushed on like a steamroller. "I'm sure I told you, we're coming tomorrow. So rearrange any plans, we are taking our baby girl to dinner *tomorrow*." Mum emphasised the last word to be sure I'd heard.

"Really, you don't have to..."

"Unless you have romantic plans? Maybe that nice looking elf who was in the paper with you…"

"No, no plans. I'll see you tomorrow," I spoke hastily, turning bright red alone on my bed. Mum had cut out that stupid newspaper photo of me and framed it.

I grimaced as I thought back to the picture. I had been captured by a cult, a dragon had been awakened and half of Cardiff Castle had fallen down above the room I had been trapped in. Unsurprisingly, the picture was not flattering. I looked dishevelled and that was underselling it.

Annoyingly, Lorandir looked attractive, even with his singed hair and Mum constantly asked if anything was going on with him. He was handsome, in a perfect elven sort of way…and you've been thinking about him a lot after that kiss, my treacherous mind added. I pulled my attention back to Mum who was detailing her and Dad's itinerary while they visited.

"…and of course it would be lovely if you could show us round the museum, and we could have a little shopping trip in town…"

"Mum," I interrupted quickly, "I do have to work you know, the shop isn't going to run itself."

"I thought Marco was helping you out?" Mum shot back, her memory for detail as keen as ever.

"Yes he is, but he only works a few hours a week and I don't like to leave him for too long. Last time I was out for a couple of hours for an appointment he rearranged my displays because he said the energy was wrong," I shuddered at the memory. I might be messy in my flat, but I am very particular about my shop and like to have things just so.

"OK. But we'll see you tomorrow, yes? We'll find you at the shop," Mum managed to sound both disappointed and determined, tonight was going to be tough.

Dad's gruff voice shouted from somewhere in the background, "I can't wait to see what you've done with it," he sounded cheerful, and in truth he was very supportive. But he was a master craftsdwarf and a stickler for detail. My throat went dry as I thought about the jewellery on offer in my shop, would it be good enough for him? I'd have to check everything and make sure Marco hadn't rearranged my displays because the flow of energy hadn't been right.

"Got to go and walk Errol, see you later."

"Bye sweetheart," Mum hung up.

Errol opened one eye sleepily.

"Well, looks like we'd better go for a walk boy," I swung my legs out of bed, purposefully pulled on some clothes and grabbed Errol's lead. After a moment's thought, I grabbed my axe too, glad that it had been enchanted to appear invisible unless people got too close. I was feeling uneasy today. My mind skittered away from thoughts about who had enchanted it.

"Get it together Amethyst," I scolded myself.

Errol growled at leaving the shop so early but allowed me to take him out to nearby Bute Park. The stone animal statues lining the walls looked at me jeeringly as we walked to the entrance. I ignored their stares and wondered for the thousandth time why anyone had thought it would be a good idea to line a stone wall with spooky realistic statues with glass eyes. I shook my head, turning my thoughts back to the phone call. Dinner with my parents. Great.

I set a fast pace and once we were past some early morning joggers, I let Errol off the lead to explore. He gave a small roar and then bounded into a flock of birds digging in the lush grass. I watched him chase the birds, leaping into the air lightly before his small wings gave up and he crashed back to the ground. His scales gleamed in the early sunlight, giving him a golden glow as he played at jumping into the air and soaring a few feet.

It wasn't that I didn't like my parents, I rationalised, they're great people, supportive, everything you could want. It was just…they expected me to be doing well…and I was…but sales weren't as strong as I'd hoped. I hadn't set up an online presence despite Aloora, my best friend and social media star, offering to help me. I sighed and tried to shake myself out of my spiralling thoughts. It was only for a couple of days. They were great parents, really.

The sounds of shouting and Errol growling brought me out of my self-absorption. A shadow fell over the park and the birds stilled. I squinted up at the large red dragon silhouetted against the sun.

There hadn't been any reports of it preying on humans since it awakened but it had made its home in the Millennium Stadium just to the West of Cardiff. A massive blow for sports fans and music lovers as it had been a popular arena as well as the crown of Wales' sports stadia, but who's going to argue with a dragon larger than a bus that can breathe fire?

As it swooped overhead, I froze, my hand resting on my axe. I had seen that dragon close up in all its scaly magnificence. In my nightmares, I still saw the jewelled eye staring at me as it devoured the cultists. I scooted under the shade of a large tree, pressing myself against its trunk in fear and tried to call Errol to me through gritted teeth. Errol ignored me and pressed himself flat to the ground, growling softly.

The dragon circled lazily then flew upwards and out of sight. The birds began to sing again. It might have been my imagination but they seemed more subdued now. I cautiously ambled over to Errol, who was still pressed against the ground and clipped on his lead before leading us home quickly. Dragons and a phone call from Mum before breakfast were more than I could take. I stopped at the Dragon's Head coffee shop on the way back to the Arcade.

Brinda was pleasant as always. "What'll it be Ame?" she asked chirpily.

"Coffee, strong please. To go…and a bacon roll…and one of those chocolate cakes."

"Och, tough morning is it?" Brinda shook her head as she pressed buttons on the shining silver coffee machine.

I grumbled about my parents coming to visit and tapped my card to pay. Brinda nodded in sympathy, her long purple ponytail bobbing as she expertly wrapped the cake into a paper bag. She pushed the bag, coffee and a hot bacon sandwich across the counter towards me.

"You can always bring them here you know," she said with a huge smile on her face, "no one makes a bacon roll like me! And the chocolate cake is to die for."

I found myself grinning back at her, "I might take you up on that." I left the shop as a couple of builders entered in their high-vis jackets, setting the shop bell jangling as they stomped in.

I always left the coffee shop in a better mood and wolfed down my sandwich as I walked. I even managed to avoid splodging ketchup down my top. Maybe today was going to be a good day after all. I chucked the last bite of sandwich to Errol. He snapped it out of the air then licked his lips before burping a small flame. I stepped sideways reflexively to avoid the fire and glanced around, grateful no one seemed to have noticed. Wyrms weren't a common pet and there were calls for them to be put on the registered animals programme. I could imagine the angry call I'd get from Uncle Owain on his wyrm farm if any films of Errol were found on the internet giving traction to that cause.

It wasn't until the second customer of the day had to get my attention away from my efforts to create unloseable jewellery that I realised what had bugged me last night about the door. The cheerful tinkle above the door as customers entered hadn't rung all morning. The bell was broken. What was going to remind me to slap on my shopkeeper's smile and make pleasantries?

As the lady left with a bracelet for her mother's birthday, I approached the door and squinted up at the bell. It was there, slightly dull and brassy but functional. Except the clapper from inside wasn't working. I got a chair and balanced on it to see clearly. I still had to stand on my tiptoes to get close to the bell. Cursing my small stature, I reached up. The clapper had been melted to the side of the bell. "What the dzrak?" I swore in amazement.

The melting point of brass is about nine hundred degrees Celsius. Thanks Dad for ensuring I knew all about the melting points of all the common metals, and most of the less common ones too.

This hadn't just been melted at random either, somehow only the clapper had been affected while the dome of the bell was intact. I had a hunch something magical had done this and grabbed my crafting goggles from their space on my shabby chic countertop.

As soon as the brown tinted lenses covered my eyes, I saw the faint traces of magic around the bell. I focused and thought I sensed leaves and growth. Elven magic perhaps, but there was a trace of something else in it. Something that reminded me horribly of the cult I had been captured by earlier in the year.

Schiztz, I thought they had all been devoured or captured. Why would anyone come to my shop? It wasn't like I had been able to stop their plans. I felt the beginnings of a tension headache so forced myself to breathe. I detached the useless bell and banged it onto my counter, chipping the white paint. The bell rolled off the counter and fell to the ground. I swore. I had artfully distressed the shabby chic countertop but this dent was unplanned. I glared at it.

Errol pounced on the bell as it rolled across the floor, easily catching it.

"Come on boy, give it here," I bent down. Errol tucked it under his chest, keeping his claws grasped tightly around the metal. He swished his tail, bent his head low and growled at me. His eyes tracked me as I feinted left then right to try to retrieve it. His growl deepened, he did not want to give it up. Great, now we were playing keep away. While Errol chewed on the bell with one side of his mouth, I retrieved a piece of charcoal from the forge. I offered it to him, just out of his reach and in his greed, he abandoned the bell, which I put back on the counter.

I chewed my bottom lip as I considered it and the strange traces of magic. If someone thought I was going to tuck my tail between my legs and run, they didn't know Amethyst Hearnson. Still chewing my lip, I immediately began sketching up some enchantment ideas to protect my shop.

Chapter 2

I was so busy sketching that I didn't notice anyone come in until a manicured hand appeared on the countertop in front of me. I looked up immediately into the clear amber eyes of Agent Jones.

"Keeping busy I see," she arched an eyebrow at me and glanced down at my defensive plans sketched out in front of me. "Had some trouble recently?"

"A girl can't be too careful," I replied before relaxing a little, "someone broke into the shop last night."

Agent Jones was immediately interested, her hand tweaked the gold bracelet around her wrist. A feline head was engraved on it, I wondered if it was a tiger, but the ears looked more pointed. She interrupted my wandering mind, "Did they take anything?"

I shook my head dragging my eyes away from her wrist, "Nothing. I woke up so I guess I scared them off." I wasn't convincing myself, let alone the formidable Agent. "They did this to my bell, have you seen it before?"

Agent Jones squinted at the bell as I turned it over to show her the clapper fused to the dome and sniffed. "Is it magical?"

“It wasn’t before, but I think magic melted it. It’s weird but I think it might be elven magic.”

“I can have the Magical Liaison Office take a look at it if you like, we’ve got experts in practically everything magical.”

“Thanks,” I replied. Agent Jones nodded, retrieved an evidence bag from her polished fake crocodile skin purse and bagged up the bell carefully before putting it into the bag.

“So…are you looking for anything in particular?” I asked, gesturing to the shop, hoping she had come to browse and not to ask for more statements.

“Actually yes,” she replied crisply, “you.”

I frowned, trying to puzzle out where this was going. “Me?”

Agent Jones nodded curtly. I got the impression she was not a lady who dealt kindly with idiots and I was trying her patience. “You. This dragon has got everyone worked up and a taskforce has been set up. We want you.”

“Me?” I said again, this time with more disbelief in my voice, “to do what? I make jewellery.” I waved my hand around the shop.

“That’s not all you do though is it, Ms Haernson.” Agent Jones raised an eyebrow at me.

I froze. My weapons business wasn’t entirely illegal but it was definitely under the counter and I thought I had been discreet enough that the authorities didn’t know about it.

She smiled and carried on, “We want you with us in case we need anything made quickly, your dwarven learnings will be valuable and you have experience with dragons after your encounter with the cult… and Aloora insisted you and her came as a “package deal”.”

I sighed. Things were making more sense now. My experience with dragons was limited to watching in terror and praying not to be eaten or cowering in parks as they flew overhead. Aloora was an expert on dragons, of course they'd want her as part of the team and of course my best friend would want me to share in her success.

"Assuming you say yes, there's a fact finding expedition coming up that I'd like you to be part of."

"Expedition? I run a shop. I can't just up and leave," bewilderment fought with indignation at the nerve of this woman.

"We would of course compensate you for your time…" That got my attention. "Would this much a week cover the expense of losing you from this valuable business for a week?"

Agent Jones had pulled a large wad of notes from her purse and skimmed a chunk off the top. How much money does the Magical Liaison Office have access to? I wondered briefly as I accepted the cash and quickly counted it, trying not to seem too eager. Agent Jones' smirk showed me I hadn't been entirely successful in not showing my glee.

"Yes, that will be adequate," I replied calmly trying to keep my composure, "and I'll just be making anything you need er…weapons wise." I clarified.

Agent Jones nodded, causing her immaculate bobbed hair to fall forward. She pushed it back deliberately then opened her handbag again. It didn't look like it was big enough to contain the dossier she pulled out but she snapped it shut before I could look more closely.

"Here are the details of the rendez-vous."

I picked the brown cardboard folder up. “Don’t believe in e-mail I see,” I quipped then regretted it as she eyed me.

“No Ms Haernson, sometimes I prefer the old fashioned method,” she frowned, “But don’t leave it lying around for thieves to find.” An odd look appeared on her face as her amber eyes scanned the shop, before she settled back into her usual in charge pose. It almost seemed like she was worried. “You’re one of mine now, I’ll send someone over to help with protection.”

“Really, there’s no need,” I tried.

“Consider it done,” Agent Jones’ tone was final, “and welcome aboard Ms Haernson.” She held out her hand. I manoeuvred the dossier under my arm to free up my hand and shook hers. Her skin was smooth and warm against my calloused hands, her handshake was as firm as I expected and I squeezed back as we eyed each other. I seemed to have passed some sort of test as she grunted and broke off the handshake.

“Call me Amethyst or Ame,” I said defiantly, “my friends do.”

Agent Jones blinked at the lack of formality. “Alright then…Amethyst, I’ve included a few items I’d like you to make for the team before we set off.”

I opened the dossier and nodded along then my ears caught up with the conversation. “Wait, who is paying for the materials for these?”

She smiled and straightened her blazer, “Just bring me a receipt and keep it honest.”

I started to bluster that I was always honest, but she was gone, her heels tapping on the hard floor as she swept out of the shop.

“What the dzrak?” I resorted to swearing again as I focused on the dossier. It was sparse on details of the expedition, just a time and place for meeting and suggested dress code – casual and easy to move in - so no cocktail dresses then, not that I owned a cocktail dress. The list of items was at the front and was the most comprehensive part of the file: gold fireproof charms, crossbow bolts, a couple of enchanted short swords, daggers…it went on. Not much then! I wondered at the choice of gold rather than a cheaper metal for the charms, then shrugged; it was her money.

I checked the date of the rendez-vous – a week’s time! My mind started whirling and I was suddenly grateful for a slow sales day as I compiled a list of components on the back of the dossier and started to plan. Sketches and component lists crowding the countertop in place of my defensive enchantment plans.

The time passed quickly and when I glanced at the large clock on the wall behind my counter, I realised I’d have to rush to make games night. Luckily it was at my best friend Aloora’s house share and I didn’t have to look my best so my superhero top and jeans would do.

I tugged on a hoody for warmth. As an afterthought, I raced upstairs and grabbed Bane. Although it was invisible to anyone who kept out of my personal space, I decided to shove it in a duffel bag – much more casual than looping it through my belt. That was my rationale anyway.

I checked on Errol. He was sleeping in the forge, snoring softly. I smiled and left him to it. He’d had a busy day helping me make a start on some of the simpler requests on Agent Jones’ list and was half way through a bucket of coal already.

As I left, I locked the door and muttered a charm over the lock, personalising it to me. Maybe I was paranoid but the thought of someone breaking in last night was creeping me out and I hadn't put any of my other enchantments in place yet.

I needed to think more carefully about what I placed where as I didn't want Errol or myself to accidentally trigger something. The personalised lock was a charm I had learned as a teenager when I kept a diary and didn't want anyone else to read my angsty thoughts.

I pulled my hood up to protect my head from the chilled breeze that blew through the city that evening and walked with pace towards Aloora's house, duffel bag on my shoulder and hands in the large pocket on my hoody. The axe handle hit my thigh through the cheap bag fabric with every stride. Maybe a duffel bag wasn't a great way to carry an axe. I would have a bruise tomorrow. I tried to vary the angle at which it hit me but that meant I was walking in a very bizarre way, part trot, part long step, wholly inelegant.

I fell into pace behind some students as we walked along Park Place towards the Student's Union. I was planning to cut through to the street behind, a slight shortcut to Aloora's place.

I couldn't help frowning at their conversation.

"So a crap tonne is bigger than a butt load." the tallest one said in a London accent.

"Agreed," said his friend, "but a shit tonne is bigger by far."

"Alright," the third one chimed in, "but is it a metric or imperial shit tonne?"

They all paused to think and I overtook them, taking care not to hit any of them with my bag as it swung wildly when I quickened my pace.

“I think you’ll find the largest measure is a dwarven dzraktun.” I couldn’t help throwing over my shoulder as I hastened away. I grinned. Sometimes I couldn’t help being a smart ass. My grin turned to a frown as the hairs pricked up on the back of my neck.

Something had changed. I looked around nervously, unconsciously drawing my duffel bag across my body in case I needed access to my axe. Then I realised what was wrong. The background noise had changed. The traffic still rumbled past but all birdsong had stopped.

Oh schiztz.

That was my thought before I saw the shadow fall across the pavement. Schiztz. Schiztz. Schiztz.

The group of students behind me gaped and one of them pulled his phone out of his baggy jeans and began filming as the dragon flew overhead.

“Run! Hide!” I shouted as I hugged the bag to my body and began to run towards the Student’s Union. The steps went up two levels, were solid concrete and, most importantly, had a large overhang that I could hide under.

The dragon roared as it swept low over the road, the sound reverberated around and I felt like my head might explode trying to contain the noise. I kept going, panting hard and staying close to the wall. A crunch of metal and tyres screeching to a halt made me turn just as I reached the safety of the steps.

The dragon had landed on a Cardiff city bus, crushing the green coach with its weight. It was on the back half of the bus, facing the back and crunched its teeth into the glass window. I winced at the sound. Other cars had unsurprisingly stopped and a smart few at the back were reversing.

Most people were crouching as low as they could in their car seats and I saw a family risk leaving the car and dashing across the road to a nearby building, huddling behind a wall.

I wanted to be surprised that a couple of drivers had their smartphones out, filming the destruction, but there were always people who would film anything. This was probably live streaming on social media right now. As if posing for them, the dragon lifted its head and roared loudly again, triumphant at catching the large bus.

The front door of the bus opened with a hiss. The dragon's head whipped round, a menacing growl rumbling in its throat.

The people in the bus were trying to get out. The dragon's full attention was now on the open doors. Smoke was curling from its nostrils and its lips curled back from its teeth intimidatingly.

My face scrunched up in indecision. I couldn't let those people get eaten without trying to help. It's not like they were cultists, just innocent shoppers riding the bus into town. Schiztz.

I unzipped the duffel bag and grabbed Bane, gripping tightly.

"Here!" I yelled, or tried to. Fear made my voice croak. I tried again, stepping from my hiding place, "Here! Dragon!"

The dragon turned its head slowly, menacingly. I waved frantically trying to both keep its attention and gesture to the people inside the bus to get out. I even mouthed the words "Get out!" as I jumped up and down on the spot.

The dragon narrowed its green eyes at me. It shifted on the bus but didn't seem to want to leave it. Its claws dug in as it faced me.

The passengers took that opportunity to pile out as quietly as they could. The group of students had stopped filming and were helping shepherd the shell shocked people to one of the nearby university buildings. A terrified lecturer was ushering people in through a red painted door.

I licked my lips as the dragon faced me. My brain raced as I tried to calculate how much time I needed to buy them and where I could hide safely assuming I wasn't killed. As that cheering thought entered my head, I realised where I'd seen this before. The dragon was acting like Errol with the mangled bell!

It clawed its scaly talons into the bus and eyed me like I wanted to take its prey, but it was too interested in the bus to actually want to chase me. I thought I could use that. I had to make it think I wanted the bus but wasn't enough of a threat for it to bother pursuing me instead of the twisted metal. With some sort of plan forming, I moved to the right. The dragon turned its neck, keeping me in its eye line. It lowered its large head, saliva dripping from between its teeth as it bared them at me. I moved back to the left, staying back and out of reach of those sharp fangs.

My plan was simple. Keep moving, make it think I was interested in the bus without getting too close and as soon as everyone was out of the bus, run and pray it stayed focused on the bus.

It seemed to be working pretty well. I weaved between cars, ignoring the eyes and cameras of the helpless passengers who gaped at me. The dragon kept its eyes narrowed and followed my movements. Hurry up bus passengers, I urged silently, glancing at the doors every time I ranged left and got them in my sights.

It was going well until a mother with a baby exited the bus. The baby started crying as it felt the breeze on its chubby cheeks and the mother desperately tried to hush it as she stood on the step by the doors and fought indecision over getting back into the bus or running for the relative safety of the university building.

The dragon heard the cry and twisted round, startled by the harsh sound. Schiztz. I cried out. The dragon stayed focused on the baby. I banged Bane on the ground. Nothing. I banged on the door of the nearest car – a sporty orange Porsche that looked like it belonged on a race course.

"Honk your horn!" I yelled. The driver looked at me like I was crazy. I probably was. The wind was blowing my hair around and I was waving a double-headed battle axe at a dragon in the middle of a main road. I brandished the axe at him and moved my hand to open the orange car door. The man shook his head, his mouth open and his mousy brown hair swaying. He pushed the locking button quickly. I widened my eyes, pursed my lips, glared, and pulled my axe back as if to break his window. Finally he pushed the centre of the steering wheel and the horn blared out.

I mouthed "Thank you," at him sweetly as he gave me an unfriendly gesture. I smiled and turned back to the dragon. The horn had worked. It was facing me and the car. I resisted the urge to stay close to cover and stepped away from the Porsche so the dragon could see me. I waved Bane high and took a couple of steps closer to the bus.

The setting sun illuminated us and shone brightly on the polished blade of my axe. By pure chance, the reflected light hit the dragon's eyes. It stretched its large wings. They flared orange in the sunlight as it flapped them and took off, the bus still in its claws.

The bus driver jumped as the bus left the ground and hastened to join the other passengers. The dragon was using its powerful wings to hover above the road. The downdraught washed over me as it stayed airborne. It lifted its head back, hissed and then opened its mouth wide.

I realised what was happening too late and dived behind an empty Vauxhall estate as it released its flames. I shouted "Sheld!" Bane glowed in my hands at the Dwarfish word. Its shield activated.

I still felt the heat as I cowered next to a tyre and watched as the flames poured across the tarmac. What an idiot. Of course it didn't need to get up to kill me. It had fire. I stayed where I was, not daring to look out. The passengers were safe, I had played my part. Now it was time to get out of here.

I deactivated Bane's shielding power and began to crawl forward, the large axe hampering me somewhat when I heard the cries of alarm. I risked looking around the car.

The dragon was flying back and forth along the road, taking chunky bites out of the bus and letting the deformed metal crash to the ground as it realised the bus wasn't meat. I saw a large piece of metal hit the front of a sedan and the car engine burst into flames as people screamed and flung themselves out of the vehicle.

I watched in horror as it made a last pass over us, swooped upwards and dropped the bus entirely. It was almost like it was in slow motion as the wreckage fell, spinning towards the ground. I tensed, and offered a silent prayer that it didn't hit anyone.

It was a miracle that it hit the steps of the Student Union. The concrete exploded downwards forcefully. Dust and rubble flew out of the impact zone. I saw a large portion of concrete hit the road a few feet from me. A few smaller chunks of concrete hit my back hard as I lay on the ground. I shielded my head with my hands, gripping Bane tightly, my knuckles turning white as I waited for the debris to settle.

The bus teetered on the pile of rubble where the steps had been. One supporting column defiantly remained standing. I looked around. Amazingly, it looked as if no one had been hurt. I huffed in relief. I debated my options: stay here and be questioned by the Magical Liaison Office or have a cold drink with my friends. I overheard someone calling the police and made my decision.

Covered in dust, I hefted Bane onto my shoulder and walked slowly through the dust cloud to Aloora's house.

Chapter 3

I knocked on the door of the shabby student rental house that Aloora shared with Marco and a couple of other housemates. I wheezed slightly from the dust and used Bane like a walking stick to prop myself up on the hundred year old Victorian tiles lining the small alcove that served as a porch while I waited.

Aloora answered the door with a smile before looking me up and down. “What happened to you?” I loved my friend, always so direct.

“Dragon dropped a bus on the Union steps,” I croaked.

Aloora frowned slightly, “That’s unusual behaviour…” she looked at a point above my shoulder. I knew she was thinking about her next podcast or social media post on dragon behaviour. Since the dragon had awakened earlier in the year, her online following as Aloora Dragonquest had spiked massively and she was enjoying the newfound audience and debates about dragons.

I coughed dramatically, drawing her attention back to me.

"Sorry. Come in and tell me all about it. What can I get you to drink?" her eyes flicked back down my dirty clothes, "and I can lend you some clothes…"

I almost laughed at that. Aloora was a petite gnome who loved tight fitting jeans and tops. Although we were practically the same height, I was a curvaceous half-dwarf. The idea of me being able to fit into any of her clothes was laughable and terrifying.

I put Bane in her ground floor bedroom and she waved me to the bathroom while she dug around her room in search of clothes. I shut the door carefully then used my hand to scoop water into my dry mouth, the tap water tasted like ambrosia. I wiped my hand over my mouth to catch some water that had dribbled down my chin then blinked as I saw myself in the mirror.

Schiztz. I looked awful. Dust covered me entirely. I looked like an extra in a student zombie film. Small pieces of concrete were stuck in my frizzy hair. I pulled out as much as I could then washed my hands and face, removing most of the grey pallor from my skin. My clothes on the other hand needed a good wash.

I stripped off to my underwear, praying that Aloora had found something decent for me to wear. She knocked on the door. I opened it cautiously; I was self-conscious about my curves despite my love of corset tops. My friend eyed me.

"Here you go," she offered me a pile of clothes she had dug out from somewhere and took my dirty ones with her.

"You don't have to wash them…" I trailed off as she gave me a look and left.

I looked down at the clothes I was now holding sceptically. I didn't have much choice, it was either put them on or have games night in my underwear, and I wasn't even wearing a matching bra and pants set. I struggled into the fluorescent jogging bottoms that Aloora had found for me and then pulled an oversized t-shirt over the top. It had an anime style dragon on it. I looked like some weird parody of a nineties rapper.

I pulled a face at my reflection in the mirror, straightened my back and held my chin up as I left the bathroom and headed to the shared kitchen.

Marco was dishing up pizza onto brightly coloured plates as I entered. He paused with his hand halfway to a plate, a slice of pizza dangling precariously from his fingers.

"What 'appened to you?" he asked, horrified by my appearance.

"Oh, you know, I've joined N-Sync," I joked.

Marco's lip curled in disgust as the cheese started to slide off the pizza.

"Watch your jeans, Marco," I nodded in the direction of the dripping cheese and plonked myself into a seat at the table, noting his horrified expression as a blob of mozzarella landed greasily on his fashionable trousers.

Aloora handed me a bottle of *Madam Mim's Cure All*. I lifted my t-shirt and rubbed some into my back where the rubble had hit me. The tincture was well known in the magical community for being able to cure practically anything, from cuts to aches and pains.

She had her smartphone in her other hand and was scrolling through social media posts. She thrust the phone into my face as

I took a swig of the cola she had put on the dented table for me.

"Is this you?" she demanded.

My eyes focused on the screen. It was footage of the dragon attack that had just happened. From inside a car, a shaky film of me running from side to side with my hands in position as if they were holding Bane. Bane itself wasn't showing up on the footage thanks to the elven magic Lorandir had worked on the axe when we were trying to prevent an artefact being stolen from Cardiff Museum.

I looked absolutely insane. The footage zoomed in on the passengers fleeing the bus and then back to me as I banged on the Porsche window. I pushed the phone away. It was strange seeing myself, especially when it had just happened and I looked like a madwoman.

I sighed loudly, "Yep, it's me, I'm sorry to say. The camera really adds the pounds huh?" I tried to joke.

"It's your ugly clothes that do that," Marco chimed in, "Why do you wear that hoody, hmmm?"

I scowled at him then brightened up as he pushed a plate of pizza towards me.

"Why were you feinting with a dragon?" Aloora persisted.

I shrugged, my mouth full of food. I swallowed, took another swig of my drink and then swallowed again. My hands traced the condensation on the side of the plain glass as I thought. I stared at the dark liquid and thought I could see the panicked faces of the bus passengers staring at me. "I couldn't let those people get killed. I had to do something."

I shuddered as I realised how close it had all been, how easily something could have gone wrong. Aloora's face softened and she reached out and patted me on my arm.

"Hey, don't worry, nothing happened. You did great," she paused and tilted her head on one side, "Do you fancy coming on my podcast? It would be great to get a first-hand account…" Aloora noted the look on my face. There was only so much a best friend would do.

"Alright, alright. Just think about it ok? I don't know what Agent Jones will say though," Aloora mused.

"Agent Jones? She came to see me today. Something about a task force. She said you insisted I was part of it."

Aloora's blue eyes shone with excitement as she nodded, "It's great right? We're going to get to go on a dragon mission and," she lowered her voice, "who knows what sort of secrets they know about dragons. What I might be able to find out."

"That's your dream I know, Ally, but why involve me? I've got the shop to run."

"I know," Aloora sighed, "I just thought it would be fun to be together on this again. We hardly see each other like we used to and this could be great. Plus I told Agent Jones you were the best at magical manufacturing and I checked Marco could watch the shop for you…"

I looked between my two friends in disbelief, "I'm going to do it aren't I?"

Aloora gave me a large smile. Marco grinned at me over his wine glass too.

I smiled back at them weakly.

"Just don't get yourself killed being a hero. I need my best friend," she joked with a playful punch to my upper arm. I winced.

"Don't worry, I'm not a hero," I replied, "just an idiot with an axe in the wrong place at the right time…and I want a favour."

Aloora raised an eyebrow at me. "My parents are coming over tomorrow. My Mum loves you Marco, please help entertain her, and you both have to come to dinner with us in the evening."

"I thought it was going to be something terrible," laughed Marco as he took another sip of the ruby coloured wine, "of course I will come. Your mama is fabulous."

I felt like a weight had lifted from my shoulders, I hadn't realised I was so tense about my parents coming tomorrow.

Then my phone rang. I answered it to a barrage from Agent Jones, "Right, what were you playing at out there? I've seen the footage, you're lucky to be alive! Why didn't you stay and wait for the authorities?! I expect a full report! Are you OK? Do you need medical attention?"

I winced, "I'm fine."

"Then you can bring a report with you when you join the task force!" she hung up without waiting for a reply. I guess I needed to write a report.

I rolled my shoulders to ease the tension out and decided to ignore that problem. I grabbed another slice of pizza and asked, "Right, what are we playing tonight?"

Aloora gestured to a pile of board games on the table.

"Idiot's pick," she grinned at me while she took a bite of pizza.

In the end, we decided on a game of Rhino Hero to start. My hands were still shaking from the adrenaline of the attack so I lost that one quickly as I knocked over the tower as I placed my second card. Then we had two games of Ghostel. Marco won both games with a convincing lead.

I called myself a taxi to take me home. It wound the long way around the city streets as Park Place was still closed. I thought I saw Agent Jones in an elegant trouser suit. She was stomping around and barking orders behind the police tape cordoning off the road.

Chapter 4

I had a fitful night's sleep, filled with dreams about a shadow moving around in my room and a dragon breathing fire while I slept. I woke up in a hot sweat, reaching for Bane which I had kept beside my bed. Errol slunk downstairs to avoid another early morning walk. I listened carefully for any noises but couldn't hear anything.

My senses heightened by fear, I crept about my small flat, turning on every light. My sparse mismatched furniture was in the same spots. Nothing had moved. I headed downstairs, getting angry that I was this fearful. That someone had made me this paranoid. I checked everywhere inside my shop. Nothing.

I flung Bane down in frustration. I had almost wanted to meet an intruder to exorcise this paranoia. The heavy axe dented the wooden floor before falling over. Schiztz.

I picked it up and heaved myself back upstairs. I was wide awake now. I decided against watching one of my favourite superhero films and instead got to work on my protection enchantments. I set up a couple of traps that would alert me if they were set off and more that would hold an intruder.

I felt a lot more secure and better for doing something rather than acting like a victim. I decided to get a celebratory bacon roll from the Dragon's Head and bribed Errol with a piece of charcoal to get him to come with me for a quick walk to the coffee shop.

Brinda was excited to see me and pulled out her phone to show me footage from last night. Schiztz, now it had made the news.

She was excited. "I must have a picture of you for the wall, now I have more famous customers!"

I glanced at the wall of faces hung on the navy walls. I couldn't imagine myself up there next to the likes of the famous elven popstar Cirian, who apparently "loved this coffee shop". I'd never seen him in here.

I wagged my finger at her as I grabbed my sandwich, "Don't make me change coffee shops when you make the best bacon sandwiches!"

Brinda winked at me as I left. I grumbled all the way back to my shop, moaning about dragons and unflattering footage to Errol. He was not sympathetic and curled up in the forge as soon as we got in.

I rolled my eyes at him and turned my attention to the plans I had made for Agent Jones' requests. I didn't have everything in stock and I'd need components fast to complete all of this in less than a week. I checked the time was reasonable and then called my go to dwarven supplier, Gunther.

He was happy to hear from me, as always. Although I suspected he was always happy to hear from his customers.

I groaned as he also brought up the video of me. Aloora had posted a link to it. I had to talk to her about my aversion to having dodgy films of me looking like I was crazy posted on the internet.

I laughed before changing the subject and rattling off the list of components I needed. Gunther paused. I could almost hear the neck rub as he considered how to obtain them and what he was going to charge me for the inconvenience, despite our friendship.

"It's for the Magical Liaison Office," I added, "no expense spared for a rush job and I need it all today."

He chirped up at that and promised to turn up later with the supplies. I smiled, at least my work would go well.

My phone bleeped with a text alert. We'll be there this afternoon treasure, can't wait to see you. Love Mum and Dad x

I smiled to myself. Trust Mum to put perfect grammar in a text message. I quickly fired off texts to Marco and Aloora reminding them of their promise for company today. Marco sent back a smiley face and Aloora replied that she'd be there after her podcast recording.

When my parents arrived mid-afternoon, neither of my friends had appeared.

Mum swept into my shop, looking put together as always with a fitted wrap dress that complimented her white hair elegantly. She was carrying two large canvas bags. I hugged her and noticed Dad behind her burdened with a third.

"Have you been shopping already Mum?!"

She laughed, "No, no, these are things for you. I'll just put them upstairs shall I?" She didn't wait for an invitation and barged upstairs. I saw some green leaves sticking out of the top of one of the bags and groaned inwardly. Despite my lack of success with keeping plants alive, she was determined to add greenery to my flat. The only thing I'd managed to keep alive to date was some Mucklewhite mushrooms – a traditional Dwarfish delicacy that seemed to thrive on neglect.

Dad and I shared a look. No doubt Mum had also bought me a couple of cheap gadgets too which she claimed would be "indispensable" to me but which inevitably I never used.

He engulfed me in a forceful hug, "How are you Amethyst?"

I returned the hug and then stepped back, "Good, good. You?"

Dad nodded, "The teaching's going ok, but you know the Dwarven Arms Council. There's so much paperwork, I'm thinking of retiring, maybe starting an online blog..."

I gaped. Dad loved teaching metalwork and was a master craftsdwarf. I couldn't imagine him quitting his teaching post or starting an online business; he still started all emails with "Dear…".

Dad moved around my shop while I listened to Mum's shoes clopping upstairs as she unloaded her bags. I watched anxiously, his approval always meant a lot to me. He paused by a couple of displays, stroking his long beard, still thick and brown despite his age.

"Nice work, Amethyst," high praise indeed from Dad, "And let me see your forge."

I gestured to the back of the shop and then followed him through the door into my workshop. Eyeing it critically, Dad's thoughtful gaze took in the tools I had left out and the mugs I hadn't washed up in the sink.

"A tidy workshop is a happy workshop," he chided softly.

"Better than the shed I had at home," I responded quickly. Dad laughed at that. My working shed had been an absolute tip when I lived with Mum and Dad. Mum wouldn't come in there and Dad had shouted at me at least once a day to tidy it up. I always claimed it was creative and refused, but I couldn't deny it was a mess.

"You've still got some things in there you know. I daren't go in but your mother's talking about turning it into a she-shed for her plants."

"It was a she-shed – my she-shed! But next time I come up, I'll sort it out. Golden promise." I held up my hand in the traditional dwarven gesture for the sacred promise.

Dad laughed at me and shook his head. He glanced around again and bent down to tickle Errol behind the ears, "Still making weapons?"

I swallowed. I couldn't hide anything from Dad. I bent under my workbench and pulled out the old army surplus bag where I kept my current stock. Dad lifted up a short sword, moving it from hand to hand and testing the balance.

"Very nice. You could teach my current students a thing or two about weapons making. No enchantments?"

"My…erm...clients... prefer a personal enchantment service, tailored for their needs."

"Smart, smart," Dad put the sword back and covered up the weapons. I hastily put them away as I heard Mum clattering downstairs.

"Those mushrooms are doing well! I've left some food in your fridge, it was nearly empty, I knew you weren't taking care of yourself. And there's a new garlic peeler I found that is amazing. I bought one for you too of course and I saw this scarf and thought of you," Mum placed a silk scarf with tiny cogs printed on it around my neck. It was lovely. Mum did have an eye for nice things.

"Er, thanks Mum."

"Now, tell me what's new with you, seen any more of that elf?" she waggled her eyebrows suggestively.

Marco arrived holding an espresso and a large cappuccino for me just in time. He gave me a wink as he passed me the coffee and started talking to Mum, distracting her effectively as he complimented her dress.

Gunther's face appeared outside the glass door. He strode in and plonked his large bag onto the countertop. It clunked as it hit the surface.

"Thanks Gunther!" I beamed, "Did you manage to get everything?"

He nodded then turned to Dad, "Dafydd! How are you? It's been too long," The two dwarves clasped hands in a traditional warrior's greeting and started catching up. I fingered the bag then heaved it into my workshop; getting my hands on the components would have to wait until tomorrow.

I walked back into the room as Mum's phone beeped. She frowned at the text message before screaming and shoving it in my face. "You're viral treasure! How amazing! Why didn't you tell me?! I had to find out from Cressida of all people! I do wish you would smarten up a bit though…"

"Ignore it Mum," I groaned, "it's nothing."

"Nothing! You're trying to fight a dragon…what are you holding?" Dad and Gunther were now crowding round the phone.

Dad pierced me with a look, knotting his bushy eyebrows together, "Why is your axe not visible?"

"Er, I had it enchanted," I stared at my shoes, examining the scuff marks on my solid boots.

"Show me." I couldn't refuse. I took Bane from its hiding place under the counter and handed it to Dad. He studied it carefully, peering along the handle and then placing his fingers to his mouth as if tasting them, "Elf magic?"

I nodded, bracing myself for a telling off. Dwarves and elves weren't exactly the best of friends even in this day and age. Dad seemed more curious than angry that I had enchanted my family's ancestral axe, "Interesting."

"That's nothing," Gunther enthused, "Ame's trying to enchant items so you can't lose them. We're close, I'm sure."

Dad looked at me, "Really? Well I suppose it could be done if you had the right enchantments, but it would work better if you could imprint it to the owner."

My mind whirled, I hadn't even thought of that. We continued debating the possibilities of crafting enchantments while Marco and Mum popped out for a shopping session in Cardiff.

Aloora turned up just after closing time with Marco and Mum. They were all laughing and Mum and Marco were carrying several bulging carrier bags. I eyed them before suggesting we head out to a local dwarven restaurant, knowing my Dad's appetite and no matter how much Mum tried, she was never quite able to master traditional Dwarfish fare.

Mum immediately criticised my drink order, “You know that the sugar in that cola will rot your teeth!”

Aloora chimed in too. I smiled and took a long swig, determined not to apologise for my unhealthy choices. Luckily Marco interrupted with a question about one of the dishes on the menu. I steered him away from ordering the tripe soup, despite Gunther’s proclamations that it was a taste sensation.

As I tucked into my plate of swarzmet, a meat dish with fat dumplings steaming on the side, Dad started grilling me on my business model. I chewed slowly, I didn’t want to admit to him that I wasn’t as successful as he hoped I was.

“Well, you know, I’m branching out a bit…In fact, I have an assignment with the Magical Liaison Office. They want my skills for a taskforce, I’m making all their artefacts. It’s a big deal.”

Mum blinked, “Well that’s fantastic news treasure! I’m so happy for you!”

“What will you be doing?” Dad asked, stroking his beard thoughtfully.

“Erm, it’s…” I blustered.

“Top secret!” Aloora saved me, “We can’t really say much but Ame’s right, it’s a big deal.”

“Well, that sounds interesting,” Dad eyed me. I turned red as if I was a teenager keeping a secret. I hated that I reverted into a child around them. “What are you doing with your shop while you’re on the taskforce?”

“Marco’s agreed to help out,” I smiled at my friend.

“Your business will be in safe hands then,” Mum cooed, “maybe you’ll make more sales too!”

"Thanks Mum!"

Dad tried to smooth things over, "Now, now, Amethyst knows what she's doing, I'm sure. We raised her to have a smart head on her shoulders. And where's Errol going to stay?"

I hadn't considered that. My face went blank, I'd assumed I could take him with me, but maybe Agent Jones wouldn't take kindly to a wyrm on the assignment. My brows knotted with worry for my pet, "I'm still working that out with the new boss…"

"Well, you know Owain would always be happy to see him," I breathed a sigh of relief at Dad's suggestion of his brother. Uncle Owain owned a wyrm farm a couple of hours away in the Brecon Beacons, that would be the perfect place for Errol if I couldn't take him with me.

The rest of the dinner passed quietly, even with Marco's dramatic announcement that he had quit acting and was moving into set and interior design. Aloora and I shared a look at that. Marco loved the arts but had dreamed of being an actor as long as we'd known him. I didn't think his move into design would last.

I promised I would get some time tomorrow to take Mum shopping and treat them both to a bacon sandwich from the Dragon's Head. I didn't mention the break-in that continued to niggle at the back of my mind, but I was a little sorry to head home alone while Mum and Dad went to their hotel.

Chapter 5

I left the shop in Marco's capable hands. He promised not to move anything while I took Mum and Dad to the Dragon's Head for brunch. I hoped it would be a relaxed meal with coffees and sandwiches. Unfortunately, Brinda had other ideas. She pushed me for a photo for the wall again and Mum overheard.

"Of course you can have a photo. Did you see this one?"

"Mu-um!" I put my head in my hands with embarrassment. It was the photo from the paper that was now apparently the screensaver for her phone.

Brinda made enthusiastic noises and before I knew it, Mum had emailed the damned picture over and Brinda was talking about framing it. Not a good start to the day.

I tucked into my sausage bap with gritted teeth. If the Dragon's Head didn't have the best coffee in the city, I would have stormed out. As it was, I kept quiet while Mum outlined her shopping plan and sought Brinda's advice on the best boutiques.

Dad headed off to Gundersson's Dwarfish Deli in the same Arcade as my shop to stock up on Dwarfish delicacies that were hard to get hold of outside the city, even for someone as well connected as Dad. I steered Mum into the shopping centre, or more accurately, she practically dragged me into every clothes shop she found.

I bought a new red leather jacket that she insisted suited my colouring. I wasn't a hundred percent sure about it but I hadn't got round to getting a new coat since the expensive woollen one I had bought on a trip with Mum last year had been destroyed by a stray wyrm pack. My backup sheepskin jacket had also had to go after it had been covered in blue slime from a goliath attack. The dry cleaner had pursed their lips when I had taken it in and, unsurprisingly, had been unable to get the goo from the giant underground carnivore out of the light coloured coat.

On the way back to the Arcade, Mum stopped outside Ambrin's in the mall. "Oh, that is lovely!" Their displays of elven jewellery were distinguished and expensive, exactly what you'd expect from the premier designer jewellers in the city. "Why aren't you making things like that?"

I winced at the unintended insult, "Erm, we have different clients Mum. They're about engagement rings and fancy watches, my customers want more day to day jewellery." Mum nodded along, clearly not listening.

I stopped talking, thinking again about my business. Did I really know who my customers were? Should I be making expensive engagement rings instead of charms? Existential questions about my shop and career choice were giving me a headache. I led the way to the cake shop in the Arcade and got us two red velvet cakes to go, a lemon drizzle as a thank you for Marco and a carrot cake for Dad.

I was barely in the door of my shop before opening the takeaway box and cramming sugar into my mouth. Schiztz, they did good cakes. Mum tutted and went to retrieve some plates from my workshop and we all stood around my shabby chic counter while we ate.

Marco talked about sales and changes he would like to make to the shop. Dad seemed particularly sold on his idea of being more Dwarfish.

"He's right Ame, I mean your logo is lovely but how do people know you're descended from master craftsdwarves?"

I frowned, I quite liked my elegant logo that just had "Amethyst's Treasures" in thin purple writing on a white background.

"I could write some ideas while you are on your mission, no?" Marco looked at me guilelessly. He genuinely wanted to help. I sighed heavily and agreed, trying not to wince at the thought of him rearranging my displays to improve energy in the shop.

Mum and Dad drove home that afternoon with Dad anxious to get home before dark. I never really understood why, but it was a family tradition that had led to us packing up before the sun was even up on one camping holiday in France to try to get back to Wales before the sun set. Mum set an embargo on waking up before 7am on holiday after that.

I spent the rest of the week negotiating with Agent Jones to allow me to bring Errol. Eventually she relented when I said I thought he could sense dragons. I also focused on the artefacts she'd asked for so I could stay in her good books. Gunther had come up trumps and all the materials I requested were in the bad he'd dropped off, along with an invoice for me to pass on to the Magical Liaison Office.

I already had some items, like the fireproof charms, in stock. Shaped like small flames with tiny cute anime faces, I enjoyed making them and they had become one of my better selling items. I repurposed some of my existing weapons stock as well to save time, but the crossbow bolts and a couple of other items I had to make speedily from scratch.

I worked hard smithing the metals with Errol's help and thanked the dwarven goddess of metalwork that I was part-dwarf, so could use my enchanting abilities to bend the metal to my will more easily.

The day of the taskforce liaison arrived swiftly and Marco had kindly offered me and Aloora a lift to the rendez-vous point near Cardiff Central Station so I wouldn't have to carry the heavy metal objects or my camping backpack.

I had grabbed a bacon sandwich for each of us from the Dragon's Head as soon as it had opened and lugged my gear to the end of the street. I enjoyed the freshness of the early morning before it warmed up fully. The weather reports were promising a heatwave this week.

Marco's old Volkswagen pulled up next to me, shamelessly parking in a no waiting zone. He stepped out, removed his designer sunglasses and stared.

"What are those?" Marco pointed at my jeans with horror.

"Jeans," I replied, "they're distressed."

Marco raised his eyebrows, "Yes they are!"

"It's a look," I muttered, although inside I knew the distressed look came from wearing them too often as they were so comfy. Marco shivered with mock horror and popped open the boot. Despite it being so early that the traffic was still sparse even in the city centre, he was looking immaculate with a neat polo shirt and fitted jeans. He even had a scarf wound round his neck that went perfectly with his top. With his tanned skin, he looked every inch a male model and I was surprised he didn't get much acting work.

I waved to Aloora sitting in the back of the car and crammed the bag containing the weapons and other enchanted items into the boot space and heaved my large backpack into the rear seats. I eased my way into the front seat. An overwhelming scent of artificial pine came over me and I wrinkled my nose at the tree shaped air freshener dangling from the rear view mirror.

Errol sneezed, a small burst of flames snorting from his nostrils, before settling down in the foot well next to my feet.

Marco raised his eyebrows at me. Aloora giggled in the back seat, the large ring on her hand sparkling in the dawn light.

"Sorry," I mumbled, "I think it's the air freshener and he didn't burn anything." I took the opportunity to remove the offending air freshener and tuck it into the glove box. Errol narrowed his eyes at me and slunk into the back seats to be further away from the stink of sickly pine. Aloora stroked his head comfortingly and retrieved a piece of beef jerky from her leather satchel for him. His tongue flicked out to take it, he always enjoyed being fed.

I handed Marco the sandwich as a peace offering and he took a large bite before swearing as some ketchup dribbled onto his immaculate polo shirt. He dabbed it with a tissue but only succeeded in mashing the sauce into his top. A stream of Italian curses left his perfect mouth.

"At least you can hide it with your scarf," I commented around a mouthful of my own sandwich. He glared at me and I shut up. The drive to the station was thankfully brief and the Today programme sounded from the car's speaker system, filling the uncomfortable silence. Marco's old radio was stuck on BBC Radio 4 and he said it helped him learn English. Normally I preferred programmes with playlists but today I was happy to listen and avoid my friend's glares.

This morning there were reports that the dragon's presence was increasing global warming as its flames heated up the surrounding air. Very localised global warming, I thought, as there was only one live dragon awake in the world and it lived a couple of miles from where we were now heading.

At the train station, I saw Agent Jones in a tailored suit, tapping her foot and looking at her watch as we arrived. I checked the digital display on the radio, we were only five minutes late.

"At last!" she exclaimed as we tumbled out of the car. She gestured to the open doors of the large grey van parked next to her. Marco kindly took the weapons and Aloora and I manhandled our bags into the rear of the van, finding space among the other bags already in there. I guessed the smart black case belonged to Agent Jones and there was an old-fashioned tapestry bag in there too. I rearranged everything so the heavy weapons were at the bottom, surprised by how light Agent Jones' bag was.

Aloora had climbed into the van and taken a single seat towards the back. It was surprisingly spacious inside. I climbed onto a two seat bench and stopped with my seatbelt halfway across my chest as I noticed another figure sitting in the badly lit interior.

“Hi,” the figure said leaning forward and rearranging the knitting on her lap, “I’m Dorothy but you can call me Dot.” The woman looked ageless, young and beautiful but somehow old as well. She reached out a pale hand with long fingers and I shook it and introduced myself. She was wearing a thick cable knit sweater despite the summer weather.

She smiled brightly, showing two slightly elongated incisors and returned to her knitting. I gulped and instinctively put my hand to my neck, wishing I was wearing a polo neck instead of the halter neck corset top I had opted for this morning in anticipation of the heat forecast for later in the day. Suddenly the choice of metal for the charms made sense. Gold couldn’t harm vampires but other metals, especially silver, could.

Aloora glared at my rudeness as the vampire sighed. “It’s alright, everybody does it the first time. But don’t worry, I use the blood banks.” She held up her hand, “I promise I won’t drink your blood. Now what’s your colours?”

“Colours?”

“Your favourite colours,” Dot held up the gold and black knitting on her lap, “I’ll make you a scarf too.”

“Cool, I love blue and silver, can you get silver wool?” Aloora leaned over to check out the scarf more closely.

“Red, I guess,” I answered, “but don’t make me a scarf, I run pretty hot, it’s the Dwarfish blood.”

Dot sighed and muttered “Lucky,” as she went back to her knitting.

Before I could ask what she meant, another passenger climbed in and Agent Jones slid the door shut hard. I bumped myself into the window seat and turned to scoot Errol along when I realised who it was. Lorandir.

He looked as elfishly handsome as before. His blonde hair was cut shorter after it had been singed when the dragon had awakened and now it looked artfully tousled. Some people spent hours in the morning trying to get hair like that. My heart beat faster and I could feel the beginnings of a blush creeping up my chest. He gave me a smile and slid into the empty seat next to me.

I glanced backwards to Aloora for help. She smirked at me and put in her earbuds in preparation for the journey. Errol sniffed Lorandir's boots then climbed into his lap, curled up and promptly went to sleep. Traitor. The elf chuckled and stroked my wyrm's head softly.

"Right," Agent Jones climbed into the driver's seat and slammed the door, "let's get this show on the road."

I finished buckling up my seatbelt and wriggled to get comfortable as it cut across my boobs. I always had trouble with seatbelts. I glared at the back of Agent Jones' head as we set off, I had a real feeling I had been set up here. I crossed my arms and stared determinedly out of the window. I wondered if I could legitimately add on an elf tax to my bill for the Magical Liaison Office.

"Hey," Lorandir's voice was soft, "how are you? I haven't seen you since…"

Since we kissed and then you left I wanted to say, but I kept my cool as I turned to look at him, "Since the cultists awoke a dragon that's now terrorising Cardiff?"

He nodded and looked nervous, “I liked spending time with you. It was fun.”

“It was fun? Nearly being killed…multiple times?! You and I have a different sense of fun!”

“I missed you afterwards.”

I stared at him indignantly, deliberately meeting his green eyes, “You know where I live; you could have called.” He looked away. Bloody elves, I almost felt sorry for giving him a hard time. Almost.

“Where exactly are we going?” I asked, turning my attention away from the elf.

Agent Jones was focusing on the road as she navigated the one way system out of the city and onto the motorway. “Avebury,” she threw over her shoulder, beeping the horn ferociously at a car which tried to cut her up.

I tried again, “What are we doing there? The dossier was pretty brief on details.”

Agent Jones smiled wolfishly, “Dragon hunting.”

Chapter 6

I tried to get more details out of Agent Jones but she concentrated on the road and turned the radio up. Nineties pop filled the van. The cheesiness of some of the songs was almost too much to handle. I went through the bag of fizzy cola bottle sweets I had bought for the journey in the first thirty minutes. I offered them round once, Aloora had her eyes closed listening to something on her phone. Dot tried one and made a face and Agent Jones and Lorandir both flat out refused to take any.

After a couple of half-hearted attempts to engage me in conversation, which I responded to with monosyllables, Lorandir put on his stylish headphones and listened to music. A glance at his phone as he was selecting tunes told me he was a soft rock fan. Not bad. I stole glances at him several times but after the second time he caught me and grinned knowingly, I forced myself to stop and focus on the rolling scenery.

As we crossed the bridge over the brown waters of the River Severn and into England, I relaxed and felt my eyes closing and fell asleep.

I snorted myself awake to find us turning off the M4. Classy I know. I snuck glances at everyone. Aloora gave me a thumbs up, Dot copied her and almost dropped her knitting. Errol growled at me from Lorandir's lap while the elf looked like he was trying not to laugh. Bloody elf.

I rubbed my eyes, scrubbing the weird bits of sleep out of the corners and blinking. I squinted at the sat nav and saw we only had about fifteen minutes left in the journey as we took a main road heading south. I stared out of the window at the tall leafy hedges that lined the road. Traffic was a little heavier than it had been in Cardiff with office goers heading out on their morning commute to whatever businesses were headquartered in the nearby towns.

The hedges gave way to rolling fields, glinting lushly in the morning sun. I saw a couple of tractors in the fields, trekking back and forth doing some agricultural activity. Road signs for local villages edged turnings off the main road with quaint names that sounded like villains or heroes in a period drama… Berwick Bassett…Winterbourne Monkton.

Outside of Avebury, large stone monoliths pierced the fields. I gaped. The town was built within a stone circle it seemed. Agent Jones turned off the main road just after a thatched country pub that sported hanging baskets filled with bright flowers. The van headed down narrower tracks, pulling to a stop on a gravel driveway outside a picturesque redbrick cottage. Roses climbed a wicker arch over a painted wooden gate. Lush herbs grew from glazed pots dotted about the small front garden, framing a paved pathway to the black front door.

Agent Jones strode up the pathway and raised her hand to the old fashioned iron handle for the doorbell. The door opened as soon as she touched the bell pull. A lady with jet black hair pulled up in a bun stood in the doorway. She looked strangely familiar but I couldn't put my finger on where I'd seen her before.

The lady folded her arms and said something to Agent Jones. Agent Jones looked like she was apologising for something. I had never seen her so uncomfortable. The lady nodded then disappeared inside.

"Right, this is where we're staying. Grab your things and let's get inside," she barked as soon as she got back to the van.

We looked at each other then grabbed our things. Lorandir picked up my weapons bag and flung it effortlessly over one shoulder with his own backpack hooked onto his other side. As he lifted it, his green t-shirt rose a little exposing his abs slightly. I had to admit, he was toned as well as devastatingly good looking, but I was still pissed that he was here and no one had told me anything.

I picked Errol up, curled him round my neck and followed the elf down the path, trying not to notice how good his behind looked in his faded jeans.

Aloora came up behind me, "Damn, he is fine, I can see why you like him," she whispered.

I gave her a look and started to hiss back a reply "I thought you batted for the other team!"

"I can still appreciate male beauty!"

Lorandir turned and winked at us. Damn elven hearing.

As we got inside, Agent Jones barked that we were to dump our stuff in our rooms and come back down for briefing. The lady of the house showed Aloora and I to a small, comfortable room with two single beds in it. Floral patterns covered the bedspreads and wallpaper, making it feel cosy and very traditional. The cream curtains in the bay window lightened the room nicely.

I peeked in the bathroom. Blue tiles carried a celtic motif across the room. There was a clawfoot, roll top bath with a single tap along the long edge. It was shaped like a gargoyle's head with the mouth hole for the water to flow from. I frowned and studied the bath more closely. The feet were definitely talon like and reminded me of Errol's claws. The large butler style sink thankfully had normal taps.

"Have you seen the wallpaper?" Aloora called. I went back into the bedroom about to tell her what I had found when she pointed at a creature next to a rose on the wall. I took a step closer. The creature that I had thought was an insect flying among the roses was a tiny fairy. Not a cute fairy from a children's book but a rather wild looking one with shaggy hair. I blinked and its wings seemed to shimmer slightly. I looked around, there were fairies all across the floral wallpaper, but no two seemed to be the same. This was strange décor. I shrugged and unpacked my backpack into the chest of drawers on my side of the room.

It didn't take long. I had brought several variations of my standard outfit; corset style tops and jeans with a couple of cardigans in case the British weather turned. I had also brought my new scarf which was now wrinkled from being scrunched into a backpack. I decided to put it on to try to air out the creases.

Errol sniffed round the entire room before jumping onto my bed. "Oh no, you're staying with me. One false move and

Agent Jones will have my guts for garters, I'm not risking you staying here alone." The small wyrm grumbled then climbed up my arm onto my shoulder. He showed his displeasure by sinking his claws in sharply before getting comfortable. I winced but I was used to my precocious wyrm.

Aloora had unpacked too, and I noted she had brought some of her costume jewellery with her. Her and my definition of "casual" were very different. "I don't think Agent Jones wears garters," she snorted.

"You never know, she might sport leopard skin underwear with suspenders," I joked. Of course Lorandir was passing our doorway just as I made that comment.

He quirked an eyebrow, gave me a smile and left the bag he had carried for me on the floor before carrying on downstairs. Dzrak!

Aloora burst into giggles and we followed him downstairs into the kitchen where the lady who I guessed owned the cottage was making tea with a black cast iron kettle on an old fashioned range cooker in the large country kitchen. Her long black dress was fitted and reminded me of a Victorian fancy dress outfit, she even had small lace ruffles on her sleeves.

I took a seat at the wooden table and snagged one of the biscuits on a decorative china plate. I was just stuffing it into my mouth when a young man I hadn't met before entered, followed by Dot.

The man had white hair in a style that I can only describe as crazy professor and he wore pleated trousers with a pressed shirt tucked into it. Definitely not casual. He marched up to Aloora and I and shook hands forcefully.

"Maximillian Baskerville! From the London Office! Communications! Call me Maxi! Pleasure to meet you Ms Haernson! And the delectable Ms Neebly or should that be Dragonquest?! Glad to be working with such fine ladies, what!" He rocked back and forth on the heels of his polished loafers as he spoke, every sentence was an exclamation.

I was a little ticked off that I had been kept in the dark and everyone else seemed to know who was on this mission. Maxi even knew Aloora's real surname. I shook his hand and was pleased to note a slight wince as I tightened my grip around his palm. Agent Jones entered the kitchen, her heels tapping on the flagstone floor. She looked around.

"Excellent, all here. We'll begin," she pushed the plate of biscuits to one end of the table and unrolled a map. I casually sidestepped my way to that end, furthest from the door and crammed another custard cream into my mouth as surreptitiously as I could manage. Unfortunately, the dry biscuit caused me to cough, spraying crumbs all over the table. So much for sneaking biscuits.

Agent Jones gave me a look. I flushed bright red. The iron kettle began to whistle loudly and Agent Jones sighed and rolled her eyes at the new interruption. The lady in black lifted it from the stove and over to a brightly painted teapot. The hot water gurgled noisily as she poured it into the pot. As she put the kettle back on an unused ring on the stove, I noticed she had nothing protecting her hands from the heat of the iron handle.

She smiled and rubbed her hands together, "You can't rush a good cup of tea, and I think we all need something to wash down these biscuits." She looked directly at me as she said that, her bright eyes twinkling above killer cheekbones. I wished the floor could swallow me up.

We waited in silence for an interminable amount of time as the tea brewed. Agent Jones tapped her foot on the floor incessantly during the silence, clearly annoyed at the interruption.

The lady poured the tea noisily through a silver tea strainer into delicate china cups perched on dainty saucers and handed them to each of us. I had never seen tea made the old fashioned way before and was used to bunging a tea bag into a mug to brew my tea at home.

She followed up with a jug of milk with a floral pattern and sugar lumps in a matching bowl with tiny tongs to drop them into the tea. I wasn't normally a fan of sugar in tea but I took three cubes for the novelty of using those little tongs.

"Keep the cups and I'll read the leaves afterwards," the lady said, as if that was an everyday thing to do. Then she stepped back and leaned against the countertop.

"Alright, thank you Mim," Agent Jones was back in command. "This map shows the stone circles and other Neolithic monuments in the county. The intelligence from the London office, thank you Maxi, says that the circles could mark where dragons sleep. What we are going to do is try to confirm that hypothesis."

Everyone nodded. I slurped my sweet tea, "How are we going to do that?"

"Glad you asked Amethyst. We've got the latest geophysical scanners from the Magical Liaison Office, that will get us started. Aloora is here to provide her expertise on dragons, their likely slumbering spots based on research she's been doing for us, and of course for translation should we come across any dragon runes.

“You and Lorandir both have experience at being in the presence of dragons so if you feel any magic or auras similar to those you felt in Cardiff, I expect to know about it.” This sounded crazy. My “experience” with the dragon in Cardiff made me want to run a mile in the opposite direction from the possibility of sensing another one.

I looked at the map to distract myself. There were two large points that represented the closest stone circles – one at Stonehenge, obviously, and one at Avebury. A number of smaller marks represented other monuments scattered across the countryside.

“We’re starting with the stone circles because that’s the best guesstimate we have right now and we want to check them out before the Summer solstice gets underway, just in case any of the cultists have ideas of awakening more dragons.”

I raised my hand, “Yes?”

“Erm, there’s a stone circle in Bute Park. Why are we in England to check out prehistoric monuments?”

“The stones in Bute Park were put there in the seventies, not when dragons were roaming the land.”

“Not the dragons we’re looking for anyway!” Maxi beamed at his own joke.

Agent Jones rolled her eyes at him. Undeterred, he coughed, held up a finger and carried on, “Stonehenge is the most famous stone circle in the British Isles! If these monuments are linked to sleeping dragons, we think its size and significance mean it’s most likely to be built on top of one! The Avebury circle is not only in a nearby location, it's also the largest circumference of stone circle in Europe! If circles have any significance with dragons, it's another likely candidate!"

"And of course, there's the legend of the two dragons," Aloora murmured. The others nodded. Since when was everyone an expert on dragons? I felt like I had been left out of some club. Seeing my confusion, Aloora continued.

"King Vortigern, a celtic king, chose a hill site for his castle in the Welsh countryside at Dinas Emrys, but it was cursed or so it seemed. Every night, the walls the masons had built during the day were torn down. Merlin himself told the king that the walls were destroyed by two dragons of fire and ice who lay beneath a lake deep underground.

"The king ordered the hill to be excavated and, sure enough, his men found a lake under the hill. They drained the lake and there lay two dragons, one red as fire and the other white as ice. Upon being woken, the dragons fought fiercely.

"The red dragon eventually defeated the other and flew off. Legend has it that it found another place to live and fell back to sleep, some say it slumbers still in a Welsh cave. There are those who say that the white dragon, though defeated, was not slain, and instead fled into the land of the Saxons, into Wessex to lick its wounds and try again to conquer the Welsh dragon when it is fully healed."

Chapter 7

"Nice story," Agent Jones commented, "but back to the mission at hand. Now, we'll have lunch here then make our way to Stonehenge this afternoon and start there, so you have the rest of the morning to yourselves. Feel free to explore the village and lunch will be at…" She looked at the lady she called Mim expectantly.

"Midday, I should think," she replied with a lazy smile, "and if you're all done with your tea, I'll read the leaves."

Agent Jones immediately stepped to the old-fashioned sink and washed her cup out before stalking out of the room. Maxi held his out to the woman with a grin. Something about the woman was niggling at the back of my mind so I stayed and listened.

"Swirl it three times first," she told him, holding his gaze with eyes so dark, they seemed black. He did as she asked and we all did the same. Then he handed her the cup. She took it and gazed into the bottom of the delicate china cup. Her eyes seemed to lose focus as if she was looking at something deeper than the tea leaves.

"Betrayal," she hissed, looking at him sharply, "but who is the betrayer and who is the betrayed?"

Maxi paled then laughed, "Such fun! You do have your ways, Mim! Bunkum of course! I'd better go check the equipment before we leave." He left the room looking unsettled.

I decided I didn't want my leaves read and made to put my cup in the sink, but the woman was too quick for me. She caught my wrist, her grip surprisingly strong, and took my cup.

"Look I…" I started. Too late.

"A warrior's heart, but you should open your mind or you may lose a chance at love." That was it. A cryptic sentence I could find in a fortune cookie. I sighed with relief. Then she looked me straight in the eyes. "You carry a powerful weapon and you will have a choice. Make the right one or you doom us all."

No pressure then. I was about to ask what she meant, but Mim had already moved on to Aloora.

"Be careful what you wish for, you might just get your heart's desire."

Lorandir was next. "You are suffering from doubt. Be open to trusting others or you close yourself to love forever."

We stood there in stunned silence at the strange messages. I didn't know about the others but my fortune didn't make sense to me. "I thought fortunes were meant to be things like 'you will meet a tall dark stranger'."

She shrugged, "I say what the leaves tell me, that's all. Besides, it looks like you've already met a tall handsome stranger…" She winked and started to leave the room when I realised where I had seen her before.

"You're Madam Mim aren't you?" I blurted. She smiled enigmatically. "Your *Cure All* is amazing!"

"Thank you, it's always nice to meet a fan." She swept out of the door.

Aloora had her head in her hands as I turned. "Could you be a bigger dweeb?" I shrugged, she was my best friend and we played board games and Dungeons and Dragons together, I didn't think either of us had a claim on traditional coolness. "Want to explore the village?"

I nodded, "Just let me make sure Agent Jones is happy with the stuff I brought her first then I'll be right with you."

I found Agent Jones in a cosy living room. Soft coloured florals adorned the sofas and chairs in this room too. Again if I looked closely, the patterns weren't quite as traditional as they seemed. I don't profess to be an expert on flowers, but these were like none I'd ever seen before. One of the twisting vines reminded me of the little shop of horrors plant; Audrey II.

A fire was laid in the large inglenook brick fireplace and Agent Jones was sat staring at the logs.

"Erm, I wanted to check if you were happy with the weapons and things I made…but I can come back later if you're busy."

She let out a sigh, "Let's have a look then. Where are they?"

She followed me upstairs to the small cosy room. She had to duck as we walked under large wooden beams over the bed. I hadn't even noticed the beams as I wasn't tall enough to worry about coming close to the ceiling.

Agent Jones opened the bag and reached for Bane. I snatched it out of her reach before she could touch it. I was protective of my ancestral axe. She raised an eyebrow at me and picked everything else up one by one. She tested the weight of the two swords I had brought. “Very nicely balanced, thanks.”

“Don’t even worry about it,” I replied casually

“And they have the enchantments I asked for?”

I nodded and pronounced the activation words for fire and ice. She repeated them back to me flawlessly. The swords responded with flashes of magic and she nodded approvingly. She pocketed the fire charms and took the large bundle of silver tipped crossbow bolts with her.

I took out the two swords and followed her out of the room. “Where do you want these?”

In the absence of any direction, I took them downstairs with me.

“Bit overkill for going round the village isn’t it?” Aloora was waiting by the front door for me, doing up a small purse that was slung diagonally over her chest. It had a dragon printed on the leather.

I didn’t bother to reply and instead put the blades point down in an old-fashioned umbrella stand in the small hallway. Agent Jones could find them later.

I checked my pocket for my phone, and made to go. Aloora shoved sun cream at me. I smiled at my friend. Thanks to my combination of Dwarfish and celtic heritage, I burned easily even in the slightest sunshine and today was going to be a scorcher.

After drenching myself in sunscreen, we headed out to look around the village. There wasn’t much to see. More sweet country cottages lined the high street through the village, a couple were thatched but most had tiled roofs. There was a typical English country church too. A stone tower reached into the sky, stretching above the lower chapel. Sunflowers lined the low stone wall and peered out from behind iron railings.

The roses and other flowers were in full bloom as we carried on past white painted cottages and brick houses. Birds sang in the lush leafy trees and bees buzzed lazily past as we meandered around the village. Errol snapped half-heartedly at one that bumbled too close to his nose. We reached the end of the high street quickly and walked back in the other direction. At the other end, we found two small shops, both empty of visitors.

One was a typical village shop, a converted building, and a little dark inside. It stocked milk, bread, ice cream, all the essentials for locals who didn't want to travel to larger towns in between their weekly supermarket deliveries. The other was a new age shop with two white wooden doors flung open invitingly – The Henge Shop. An appropriate name. Books about crystals, ley lines and energies lined the shelves along with tourist guides to Avebury and Wiltshire. There were displays from local craftspeople too.

While Aloora scanned the books, I perused the shelves, appreciating the techniques used in the pewter, ceramic and even pebble jewellery. There were mostly celtic designs, with spirals and trees of life hanging from silver chains. Hares seemed to be popular too.

I selected one of the pebbles with a flowing horse on it for Dad. For Mum, I chose a tea towel with the same horse on it and several others. Apparently there were white horses carved into the chalky soil across Wiltshire. That sounded like the sort of road trip Mum would enjoy, she was always looking for panoramic views and walking holidays.

I walked past the colourful display of new age angels next to cheerful scarves and summer bags towards the till. Errol growled at a carved wooden dragon as we passed and I soothed him with my free hand, ensuring he stayed on my shoulder. I didn't fancy paying for breakages.

I stopped as I saw a selection of lotions and potions in green bottles with Madam Mim's face on them. I picked one up and studied it, *Luscious Locks Lotion – apply daily for best results – all natural ingredients*. I turned it over, there were instructions but no list of ingredients. My hair was thick and bushy so I decided to give it a miss. I didn't need extra volume.

Then I spotted the stones. Fossils, pyrite and sparkling geodes crowded for space along wooden shelves. A giant polished ammonite partially blocked a door marked "staff only".

Glass bowls and cocktail glasses glinted under the lights and held minor gemstones and minerals in a blaze of colour. I picked up bright red jasper, enjoying the flecks of black that enhanced its beauty. There was green marbled malachite, clear calcites and I was entranced by the polished stones. I selected a few, including one unpolished stone with hints of blue mineral sparkling through the rough surface and took them to the till. I would enjoy working these into my jewellery.

The blonde lady smiled at me and reached out to tickle Errol under the chin. She asked if I wanted a bag as she scanned barcodes and did some mental arithmetic for the stones I had chosen. I nodded and she upsold me a canvas bag with a line drawing of Avebury stone circle on it.

As she carefully placed my items into the bag, she got a faraway look in her eye and then selected a small dark purple stone from the shelf behind her. I recognised it as an amethyst, my namesake jewel. “This is yours.” she said and placed it in the bag.

“Erm, thanks, how much is it?”

The lady smiled, “It is not for sale.” I looked at her, confused. This was a sales technique I hadn’t heard of before. She laughed, a melodic sound that echoed through the wind chimes over the door. “It is a gift. For protection.”

She handed me the bag and I felt very touristy and confused as I left through the second door, blinking at the sunshine.

Aloora joined me soon after, beaming and carrying a couple of books about the henges and one she had found on dragon mythology in Wessex. I stuffed them in my newly acquired bag so she wouldn’t have to lug them around and we pondered what to do with the remaining hour before lunch.

We decided to skip Avebury Manor, the National Trust House, in case it took too long and instead popped back into the village shop for an ice cream before we wandered around the stones.

I bit into my chocolate covered ice cream as we walked through the gate to a field littered with large monoliths. It was as if a careless giant had tossed rocks around the village and by luck they hadn’t hit any houses. Aloora and I were the only ones in the field on this weekday and we roamed across it, posing for photographs by the large stones.

I was amazed that we could walk right up to the stones and touch them. The cynical part of me was also a little amazed that no one had written graffiti all over the boulders, I guessed that was the difference between country and city living. If there was a giant monolith in Cardiff city centre, someone would have scrawled on it, or balanced a traffic cone on top of it. I voiced my thoughts to Aloora who laughed.

She was carefully pacing across the gaps between the stones, trying to guess where a dragon would likely be, if there was one underneath the green fields. I finished my ice cream and wandered from stone to stone. I looked around furtively but there was no one to stop me, so I reached out and touched one. It was warm and somehow felt comfortable under my hand as if it was an old friend.

I rubbed it for luck and traced a small indentation with my hand, "What are you and your friends hiding?" I whispered. I thought I felt it vibrate slightly under my hand and drew back in shock. Errol grumbled at the sudden movement then climbed down. I looked around. Aloora was now lying on the dry grass, pressing her ear to it. There was no one else around so I let Errol go chasing grasshoppers in the grass.

I pressed my hands to the rock again and this time leaned my ear to it. Nothing. Some dwarves have an affinity for stone, others don't. My family's affinity has always been for metal, it's part of the reason I went into jewellery making and weapon smithing. I wasn't surprised I couldn't feel anything from the rock. I didn't know anything about the composition of the henge but inanimate objects didn't usually vibrate when I touched them. That was weird.

I tried one last time with that stone. Nothing. I moved to one of its neighbours. Nothing. Aloora reminded me of the time and I called Errol to heel. I touched all of the stones on the way back, trying to recreate the sensation I had felt earlier. I left the field disappointed and we walked down the dusty high street in silence towards Madam Mim's cottage.

I reached up to pull the cast iron door pull and Madam Mim opened the door before I could touch it.

"Does this thing even work?" I asked with a smile. She smiled back at me, turned and walked across the flagstone floor to the kitchen. I looked at Aloora, who shrugged and followed her. I left my canvas tote bag by the umbrella stand and joined them in the kitchen.

The large wooden table was crammed with cold meats and cheeses. Fresh looking salads and fruits in glazed bowls were dotted around the table. Smaller dishes of olives and pickles fit in between them snugly. A large wooden chopping board held chunky slices of fresh bread. My mouth started watering instantly, it looked so appetising. I plonked myself onto the only free chair, between Madam Mim at the head of the table and Aloora to my right and began piling food onto my plate, scooping some into an empty bowl for Errol to eat on the floor.

Aloora chattered away about the stones and the books she'd brought. Agent Jones asked if she'd seen any sign of dragon runes. I focused on eating my ham, cheese and pickle doorstop sandwich. In between bites, I decided to try to find out more about our host.

"So, I didn't know you lived here."

"It is not my home, so much as where I am needed now. I am happy to be called to this sacred place."

"Oh, where is your home then?"

"I've been most places around these isles, but I was born in Wales and made Glastonbury my home away from home. My shop is there and it's where I develop all my recipes."

I nodded, "I saw some of your range in the Henge Shop, I had no idea you did so much. My gran always had your *Cure All* at home, she doled it out for everything!"

She laughed, it sounded like water babbling in a brook or a warbling bird, "That has been by far and away my most popular creation, I've never been able to better it. The gift from the shop is valuable, you know that?"

I took a bite of my sandwich to buy me some time to process that she knew the shopkeeper had given me a jewel, "It's certainly a lovely piece of amethyst, but it's not the most expensive jewel I've ever held." I replied not willing to commit to more.

"Dwarves," she sighed, "always thinking about gold. No, it is valuable in other ways. Do you know the properties of stones?" I nodded, I remembered learning about them at school, alongside maths and mining techniques. "Then you know that amethyst is a powerful protector as well as a healer and purifier. It can rid negative thoughts and promote positivity. Keep it with you and you will be protected."

I took another large bite. I had no idea what to say to that. Lorandir replied for me from across the table, "I can believe that Amethyst is all those things, a valuable jewel indeed."

I frowned. I had the feeling I was being made fun of, "Actually, amethyst is an incredibly common gemstone. In fact, it's one of the few stones whose value isn't determined by size or carat but by the depth of colour and clarity."

I didn't want to hear a reply so I stuffed the rest of the sandwich into my face, grabbed an apple and made an excuse to check on my things before we left. Agent Jones shouted after me that we would be leaving at thirteen hundred hours exactly.

I sat in my room and stared at the jewel, moving it from hand to hand and stroking it. It was the darkest purple I had ever seen and it was beautiful. I thought about how I would mount it back at my workshop. I thought a necklace would work well, or a bracelet, perhaps in a celtic style cuff like the jewellery at the Henge Shop. For now, I decided to "open my mind" as Madam Mim had suggested in her fortune telling and carry it with me. What was the worst that could happen? I slipped it into my pocket, grabbed Bane and walked downstairs to sit in the living room until thirteen hundred hours, whenever that was.

Chapter 8

Thirteen hundred hours meant one pm apparently. As the antique clock on the mantelpiece chimed, Agent Jones strode into the cosy living room to find me playing on my smartphone, Aloora curled up in an armchair reading one of her new books, Dot still knitting her scarf and Lorandir lounging in the self-assured way that comes naturally to elves.

She was still carrying her mock crocodile handbag, and was now dressed in linen trousers with a light tank top, looking put together as always.

Maxi huffed into the room carrying a large, bulging rucksack. "Got the equipment!"

Agent Jones nodded and handed out fire charms to Maxi and Dot. I had attached them to key chains and there followed a couple of minutes as they worked them onto their existing keyrings. Lorandir refused the charm offered to him, “I still have mine,” he said, looking at me.

I shrugged. I hadn’t asked for them back after our adventures earlier in the year. Aloora grinned at me and flicked back her hair, showing off the fire charm earrings I had made for her, a little showier than my usual style to go with her costume jewellery. I had made myself earrings too and tilted my head in answer.

Agent Jones picked up the two swords from the umbrella stand and strode to the van. We all scrambled to follow her. I made sure I sat next to Aloora this time.

The drive to Stonehenge was only about forty minutes but the warmth of the van, coupled with my full belly lulled me to sleep before we’d made it through the next town. I was woken by the sound of screeching and a feeling of being flung forward as Agent Jones slammed on the brakes. Errol hissed as he was flung from my lap.

“What the…?” I blinked and looked around. Everyone was tense and trying to see out of the dark windows. I looked too, and it took me a minute to process what I was seeing.

Huge black spider-like creatures out of nightmares crawled in front of the van, blocking our path. I stared at them. Each one was as large as a horse but nowhere near as cute. Instead of scuttling onwards on their ten legs each, they stopped and turned towards us. Their many purple eyes glinted in the afternoon sun and yellow venom glistened on their very large, very obvious mandibles. They began to swarm towards the van, surrounding it in a wide circle.

“Schiztz! What the dzrak are those?” I whispered, reaching instinctively for the comfort of having Bane in my hands.

“Araneae Theraphosidae Horribilus. Tarfangtulas,” replied Lorandir.

“Apt,” muttered Aloora as she looked at them with wide eyes.

“They’re normally contained in the fae realm or the woods around Breconia…” the elf continued, naming the elven city in the Welsh countryside.

Agent Jones rubbed her hands together, “Well I don’t think they’re going to tell us why they’re here. Buckle up everyone!”

We were already wearing seatbelts, but I made sure mine was tight before placing Bane under my seat and grabbing Errol close to my chest.

Agent Jones revved the engine and then accelerated hard, aiming between two of the hideous creatures. The van almost made it. The spiders were knocked aside. The van jolted. I heard a fleshy crunch as the tyres rolled over legs. But the tarfangtulas were fast. Seeing us escape, they swarmed to the van. Two jumped onto it, leaping high into the air and landing with a bang on the roof. Dents began to appear as their legs found purchase. Another climbed the side, treating me to a close up view of its nightmarish face. Ten purple eyes looked in at the window. It opened its jaws and tried to bite through the glass. Yellow drool streaked across the window. I leaned backwards into Aloora, who was also leaning backwards, trying to get away from the viscious spider.

Having failed to bite through, it climbed onto the roof with the other two, heaving its large hairy abdomen up the side of the van. This close, I could see that it wasn’t black as I had first thought but very dark blue, almost iridescent. Bristling hairs covered its body. The blue faded to white at the tips of its legs, which ended with a single claw on each of them.

Agent Jones was struggling to make headway as another tarfangtula had climbed onto the windscreen. "Hold on!" she shouted before making a handbrake turn. The van screeched in protest and the spiders were shook off. She started driving back the way we had come, down the wrong side of the road, but it was clear we wouldn't get away from them. She turned sharply again then pulled the vehicle to a stop.

Errol scrabbled at my chest, scratching my arm as he fought to get free. As soon as I let him go, he dived under a chair in fear. I didn't blame him.

Agent Jones breathed out as she formulated a plan, "OK, Dot, grab a sword and get outside. Maxi, get one of the crossbows and open a window. Take whatever shot you can get. Someone needs to drive, so I can shoot." She bent down and retrieved a crossbow from the glovebox.

"I can enchant the bolts," I blurted.

She nodded at me, "OK, fire should do it, I need it done yesterday!" She tossed me a bag of bolts. I moved my hands over them, allowing my natural magic to flow through my hands. I repeated the Dwarfish words for fire, incineration and flame, concentrating over each bolt before placing it next to Agent Jones or Maxi. Each of them shot the crossbows with pinpoint accuracy, unloading bolts into the creatures' eyes.

But the crossbows were slow and the spiders weren't dying. They lurched from side to side in pain and anger as they tried to shake the bolts loose before pressing the attack.

Aloora switched into the front seat nervously. She had only passed her test last year and was now about to drive us through a horde of murderous spider things. She waited for a gap, hands tensed on the steering wheel.

Dot had jumped out of the van, leaving the door open. She whirled the sword like an expert and moved inhumanly fast as she raced through the spiders, dodging clawed legs and fangs. She jumped over one of the creatures and landed on its back, plunging the sharp blade into it. She must have picked the ice blade; I saw the frost spread across its back as it fell to the ground. One of the bolts Agent Jones loosed exploded upon contact with a spider that Dot was close to. She yelled and fell back in surprise. I may have gone overboard with some of the enchantments.

Lorandir jumped after her, shouting to activate the shield on his sword. I had enchanted it for him when we had first met. The tarfangtulas pressed up against the magical shield. They reared up and crashed down using their full weight as they tried to break it. I was pleased to see that it held; but it had a time limit. Lorandir used his elven agility to run through the spiders. Not to be outdone by a vampire, he leapt from one to another, plunging his sword into their heads. I saw the glow of the runes on the blade activate as he yelled the Dwarfish words. I noted with professional satisfaction that his strikes were fatal more often than not. The true strike rune I had embedded in the sword must be working. He let off a blast of magic, sending two spiders flying into the air. They landed on their backs with force and only one got up again.

It looked like we were winning…for a moment.

"Drive!" yelled Agent Jones as she unloaded another bolt into the mouth of one of the spiders. Aloora tried to drive off with the handbrake still on and then stalled. As she panicked, one of the creatures pushed its legs into the van through the open side door. I threw the last of the bolts to Maxi and grabbed Bane from where it had fallen under the seat.

The thing manoeuvred itself to look into the van as it struggled to get purchase on the metal floor. It snapped its mouth open and shut, uttering a guttural shriek that made my skin crawl. Aloora screamed as she tried to turn the keys and get into gear. Maxi loosed a crossbow bolt almost at point blank range into the largest of its purple eyes. It shrieked in pain and turned to face him, snapping its jaws at the crossbow and wrenching it from his grasp. Agent Jones twisted in her seat to try to help. Her hand was glowing slightly. I noticed a familiar dagger forged from a dragon fang in her hand. She drove it into the side of the monster's head, causing it to scream again. If anything it made the thing angrier.

My fingers closed on my axe and I swung at the hairy leg closest to me, connecting hard. Bane glowed in my hands as the blade bit deep into the tarfangtula's leg. Hot yellow liquid sprayed out, splattering over my face and neck. It burned where it struck me. I cried in surprise. I untangled my scarf from around my neck and used the dry end to wipe the goo off of my face. The burning dulled to a tingle and I dropped the scarf on the ground.

The yellow blood continued to ooze from the wound. The creature stumbled and turned its attention to me. I whispered to activate Bane's shield, just as the monster lunged forward, getting another leg into the vehicle. I gestured to Maxi to get close to me as I moved forward, testing if I could push the giant spider out using the shield. He drew his own sword and activated the fire rune I had charmed into it. He jabbed at the creature's hideous face as he moved across the chairs.

The thing shrieked again and moved back a little before lunging for us again. I heard the welcome sound of the engine starting. I turned my attention to the battle outside. It looked like Dot and Lorandir were winning but there were still too many tarfangtulas crowding around the van for my liking. They poured towards us. An angry chittering came from their disgusting jaws. Agent Jones swore as one crashed into the van. The vehicle rocked perilously.

A flash of inspiration came to me and I bent down to touch the metal floor of the vehicle. I reached inside for my magic and felt it flow out of me into the van. I traced the Dwarfish rune for fire onto the floor as I spoke the words to enchant it. The rune blazed with flames and then the van did the same. The creature attacking Maxi and I stopped trying to get into the van and instead backed out of it fiercely, shrieking again as the fire came into contact with its body.

Agent Jones looked at me with shock, the flames leaving us all unscathed thanks to the fire proof charms I had created. "Get into the van!" she shouted at the two warriors outside. Aloora drove us forward directly into the remaining spiders that gathered to block our path. I braced myself for impact as the vampire and elf leapt into the vehicle. The spiders shrunk away from the flaming van and we passed through.

As we drove, Lorandir leaned out of the van and let off a blast of magic that shattered the remaining monsters.

My jaw dropped, "Why didn't you do that in the first place?"

"I didn't want to accidentally hurt any of you," he shrugged nonchalantly.

"Stop the van!" Agent Jones ordered the trembling Aloora. My best friend nodded, stopped the van sharply then got out and promptly vomited.

Agent Jones was already on the phone to someone, talking about containment and cleaning up a mess. That was one way to describe a dzraktun of oversized arachnid corpses littered across a main road.

She hung up and looked at us. "Right, Dot, you stay here and wait for the clean-up team. I've called Mim as well so you'll have company and she can ward the area while we wait for official roadblocks. Is anyone injured?" Miraculously, everyone else shook their heads.

I reached self-consciously to my face, stained yellow from the spider goop and still tingling. Lorandir stepped close and reached a hand out to my cheek in an intimate gesture. I nearly stepped away but forced myself to stay still and let his healing magic wash over me. The sensations of dark chocolate, honey mead and running through a sunlit forest washed over me as his aura entangled with mine. He stepped away and I was left with my eyes closed and my lips slightly parted. The tingling had stopped, but judging by what I could see on my top, the yellow stain remained. Great.

Agent Jones squinted at us, "OK, so the rest of us will carry on as planned...carefully. Those spiders weren't here by accident, someone planned this." She glossed over the part about someone trying to kill us with giant arachnids. "Is the equipment still alright Maxi?" I looked around. Was I the only one who had clocked that someone had sent the creatures after us?

Maxi bent his head into the still alight van and then gave a thumbs up, “Yah, all good.”

Everyone was so calm after nearly being killed that I wanted to ask if this was a standard day for the Magical Liaison Office and if there was danger money but Agent Jones interrupted my thoughts, “Amethyst! Get that fire out before the van explodes! We are supposed to be incognito here!”

I rushed over to the vehicle and deactivated the rune. Idiot. I hadn’t even thought of the fuel tank! The charred outline of the symbol remained on the floor. I scuffed it with my boot but the burn mark stubbornly remained. Looks like I’d enchanted the van permanently.

Chapter 9

Dot swapped swords with Maxi and set about burning the corpses as the rest of us drove off, Agent Jones firmly back behind the wheel. I noticed her staring hostilely out of the window. “Bloody portals,” she muttered to herself. I followed her gaze to a crop circle carved in an intricate pattern into a nearby field of wheat. The edges looked scorched as if a massive burst of energy had been expended.

I turned back to my friend. Aloora sat hunched up by the window, trembling in shock with Errol curled up on her lap, giving her his warmth. I handed her pieces of a chocolate cereal bar that Agent Jones had fished out of her bag and patted her arm. I was awful at handling emotions, especially in other people.

There wasn't another car on the road as we sped to Stonehenge and I commented on it. Maxi frowned, "Protocol is to say there's a bomb scare in such situations, but I didn't notice any traffic before the Araneae Theraphosidae Horribili showed up either!"

"Nice use of Latin plural for the spiders," Aloora grinned at him, sounding a little more like her normal self. I smiled at her, but didn't try to guess at what she meant. My friend was too smart for me, especially where linguistics was concerned. One thing did bother me though.

"Massive spider attacks happen often enough that there's protocol?!"

He shrugged, "Attacks by magical creatures, code 1001. Protocol is to contain and distract the press, civilians and politicians by announcing a bomb scare." He sounded like he was reciting from a manual, "The clean-up vehicles all look like explosive response units too!"

I stared at him and was about to say something witty in reply when my phone rang. I pulled it out of my pocket and glanced at the number. "Marco, what's up?"

"Hi Ame, how is your trip?"

I thought about the spiders and decided to spare him the details, "Eventful. How are things with you?"

"The designs are going great, I think you will be very happy. Your Dad loves them."

"What? My Dad is there?!"

He laughed, "No, no, do not be silly. I have sent pictures."

"How did you get his number? No wait, don't worry about that. Why haven't you sent me any pictures?" I could feel the tension starting to rise in my shoulders and I rolled them slowly backwards, taking deep breaths.

"It will be a surprise for you!" I breathed again, not trusting myself to say anything. I hate surprises. "But I am not calling you for shop designs, there is a man here."

"And?" I replied blankly, "Does he want to buy anything?"

"No, he says he is from Magical Liaison Office," Marco elongated each word carefully as if reading it out, "he says he has wards to set up in the shop. I thought I should call you."

"Hang on." I put the phone on my chest, reached forward and tapped Agent Jones on the shoulder, "There's someone who says they're from Magical Liaison at my shop setting up wards."

Agent Jones nodded, "That would be Smith."

I put the phone on speaker, "What's his name?"

"Agent Smith."

"What does he look like?"

I could almost hear Marco looking the agent up and down, "He is short, blonde, baby blue eyes, green skin, nice suit…"

I saw Agent Jones smile, "That's him," she called loudly over her shoulder while still driving, "Let him in Marco, he's putting in more protection for the shop."

"OK." Marco hung up. I looked at the handset in disbelief, this was my business, my shop, my home and it looked like I didn't get a say in anything anymore.

"Don't worry, Smith's great, he's the best in Wales for wards and protection spells," Agent Jones reassured me. I huffed and took my own bite out of the chocolate flavoured cereal bar.

We arrived at Stonehenge soon after and pulled into the visitors' car park. Maxi checked the equipment and lugged the backpack onto his shoulders. I debated whether to take Bane as we left the van and decided to bring it on principle.

A modern building with a curved roof supported by large metal poles squatted near the car park. Agent Jones told us to start walking across the fields on a well-trodden foot path while she spoke to the staff. We walked towards the stones in the mid-afternoon sun. Errol prowled through the grass chasing grasshoppers and other small insects, his red back glinting in the sunshine.

It was an odd sensation as we approached the henge. I had an overwhelming sense of history and of something much bigger and older than any of us, but it was so close to a road that it felt like it was somehow mixed with modern times as well. The grass was a dusty yellow in the summer sun and the stones rose out of it like an ancient monument, seeming to change colour from butter yellow to grey as they reflected the light.

As we approached, I felt dwarfed – pun not intended – by the henge. The monoliths were enormous and arranged in a sort of semi circle with others lying on the ground where they had fallen during the march of history. In the middle of the circle were several large upright carved boulders, some with horizontal stones on top. I can't explain it, but the stones seemed to have a sort of energy and I felt that this was a sacred place.

There were very few tourists around, and they were all posing for photos with the stones in the background. I decided to join them and snapped a few pictures with my smartphone as we got closer. Maxi had some sort of selfie stick with him and got a good one of the four of us and Errol with the henge looming behind us.

We paused to wait for Agent Jones. The tourist route was clearly marked and didn't allow us to get too close to the stones. I wondered aloud why that was and Aloora answered, whispering as if she too felt that this was a sacred place.

"English Heritage put a stop to people going too close to the monoliths as everyone was touching them and causing too much damage. Now it's only on the winter and summer solstice that special groups are allowed into the henge itself, for religious festivals."

I nodded along. I'd seen the scenes on news reports in previous years of druids of all races wielding crystal staffs and wearing long cloaks as they celebrated amongst the stones alongside humans in some sort of significant ritual.

Agent Jones walked up to us, with a tall gangly man trotting to keep up with her stride. "Right, the visitor team have remembered that they did give us permission to carry out this survey today and Roger here is going to supervise and keep any tourists out of the way." She nodded over her shoulder at the man in khaki trousers and an English Heritage t-shirt who had his arms crossed and looked less than pleased that we were doing this survey.

"I still don't understand the urgency of this, we've had geophysical surveys before obviously, and all archaeological finds are detailed in the visitor centre…"

Agent Jones cut him off, "And as I've explained repeatedly, the government has been given some information about a find in this area and has sent us to investigate now. Maxi, get the equipment ready and let's get going so we don't have to keep Roger after closing time."

Maxi pulled out radios for each of us and four large electronic devices from his backpack and gave one to everyone except me. I was slightly miffed that I didn't get one but at least I couldn't mess up a survey if I wasn't taking part. He clipped his own radio to the shoulder strap on his backpack and then talked us through the more unusual devices.

"These are the latest in ground penetrating radar, they use radio waves to penetrate the surface and show what's underneath, what! These have been modified to extend beyond the usual range and show magical artefacts that may not show up using traditional methods!"

Roger's eyes widened at the last statement and I tuned out and gazed at the awesome stones as Maxi started to describe the frequencies that the devices worked at. Aloora elbowed me in the ribs as he got to the part about how to work the things.

"So, all you do is turn it on here! Then we'll walk around the site, in straight lines! This will build up a picture! I don't expect you to read the screens as you go, but if you see anything odd, use the touch screen here to mark it like this!" He jabbed his finger at his screen and a red circle appeared. He showed us how to erase the mark by repeating the action.

"The key is to go slowly, yah! The machines need time to gather the data!" He then demonstrated the snail's pace we had to go at before turning back to us and beaming. "We'll split up so we can cover the most ground! Amethyst and I will take the henge itself, what! The rest of you will pace the outside and we'll see what we can find! Meet in the middle with us when you're done!"

Roger wasn't so easily defeated, "We don't allow wyrms on site outside of the designated religious festivals, pre-agreed with the site." He crossed his arms.

Errol, with unfortunate timing, chose that moment to leap onto Roger's boot, grabbing a large green grasshopper in his mouth. He chewed it slowly and drooled onto the brown leather. Roger looked horrified. I bent and scooped him up.

"He's got special senses that help with the, erm, geophysics. He's very…attuned…to the radar frequencies," I lied.

Agent Jones smirked at me. Roger looked dumbfounded. Maxi handed me a smaller device and turned, leading me towards the towering stones before there was a chance to reply. As we walked towards the henge, my skin was tingling as we neared the stones. I was awestruck as they towered over me. It was the closest to a religious experience as I'd ever had.

"Awesome aren't they?! I thought you'd be best for this because of your heritage. Are the stones speaking to you?!"

I squinted at him, trying to decide if he was joking, then put my hand on the closest stone. It was warm and rough against my skin in a comforting way as if it were the most solid and stable thing in the world. Given how long these stones had been here, maybe it was. I strained my senses, but any magic in them was beyond my powers to find. Ruefully and reluctantly, I removed my hand and shook my head.

Maxi beamed, "Technology it is then!" He pointed to the smaller device and leaned in to turn it on, "This will pick up the smallest traces of magic in the stones and scan them inside! Press this button when you start on a new stone, then this one when you finish! The GPS will update the position so we can work out which is which back at base camp! When you get to the stones with horizontals, you can do the whole structure in one scan, what! You do that while I work the ground!"

He began pacing around the stones in an ordered fashion, starting with the middle stones and working outwards, focused on the fuzzy radar screen and every so often stopping to jab something on the screen with his finger. I was glad we wouldn't be talking much, it was exhausting dealing with so much blustering enthusiasm that he exclaimed everything.

I pointed my device at the closest stone, pressed the green button as instructed, and moved it slowly up and down, taking in the entire length and breadth of it. There was a small screen on the handheld machine, it swirled in black and white as I moved it up and down the stone. I had no idea what that meant. Once I was sure the stone had been completely mapped, I pressed the red button and moved to the next one, pressing the small green button to indicate it was a new stone.

Errol seemed to realise he had caused trouble as he stayed by my feet for the first couple of stones, uncharacteristically at heel. As I scanned a stone that had fallen and embedded itself in the ground, the wyrm decided to climb it and sun himself arrogantly on the warm rock. I hissed at him to get off but he rolled over and stretched out.

My choices were: climb on the rock myself or ignore him and try to call him back later. I glanced over to where Roger was standing, arms folded, glaring at Agent Jones and decided against antagonising him further where Errol was concerned.

"Stay there then!" I ordered. Errol gave a soft snore. At least I knew where he was and he was unlikely to cause any trouble asleep.

I scanned my first trio of stones next. Two large upright shaped boulders supported one carved horizontal stone. It was masterfully done to have stood for so many thousands of years. The screen on my machine swirled in technicolour for the first time as I slowly moved the device around to map the entire structure. I tapped the screen a couple of times but nothing changed so I shouted to Maxi. Trust me to break the equipment!

Maxi strode over calmly like he dealt with tech support all the time. I showed him my screen and he started rocking up and down on his feet, visibly more excited than usual. "Amazing Amethyst! Well done!" he clapped me on the back like I had personally done something awesome, "This shows traces of the original magic still in the stones! Can you feel anything?"

Maxi's enthusiasm was catching. I handed him the machine and stepped towards the stones, my hands out in front of me. As I touched them, the warmth of the rock seemed to reach out to me, filling my senses. It was like nothing I had experienced before. I felt like I could talk to the stones, like they were living things. Suddenly I knew that they were made to be worshipped, that this was why dwarves lived underground to be close to stones such as these.

I wished I had brought my goggles with me to see the aura around the monoliths. I felt a slight vibration start under my hands as if answering my excitement. I looked back at Maxi.

"Well?! Is it like the standing stones at Piccolo San Barnardo? I had a religious experience there on my gap yaah…it might have been the vino I'd imbibed though, strong stuff!"

"Can't you feel it?" I asked, caressing the warm stone with my hands as I tried to take in more of the magic.

"I think you should stop now!" Maxi replied, taking a step back and looking worried.

I laughed. I felt powerful.

"Your eyes are glowing! I think, I think you should take your hands orf the stone!" Maxi took another step back, reached down to his radio and muttered something.

"What are you talking about?" I laughed again, I had the insane thought that I could move the stone if I wanted, that it could respond to my thoughts. Power crackled through me like electricity, I could feel it flowing across my skin and I felt my hair rising out.

Errol chose that moment to jump off his warm rock with a growl and crawl up my leg, his claws scratching through my worn jeans. I took my hands off the rock to push him off and felt the power leave me. I suddenly felt dizzy. Errol was looking between the rock and me, still growling. I sank to the ground and reached out to comfort him.

Maxi looked at me, his hand still on his radio, "Stand down!"

I looked around. The rest of the team had stopped their scanning and were looking at me. Lorandir's hands were glowing green as he pulled magic towards him. I noticed movement on the ground and looked down. Tendrils of vines were disappearing from the floor. I stepped on one spitefully and ground my boot onto it, annoyed at myself for getting caught up in whatever that was and annoyed at my team for trying to restrain me.

"What was that?!"

“No idea, it felt…weird.” I didn’t want to describe the feeling of absolute power over the henge I had when I connected with that stone.

“I’ll have to file a report later…are you ok to continue scanning?” Maxi was obviously worried and not his usual confident self.

I waved it off, “Of course, hand me the device and let’s keep going. Don’t want to keep Roger waiting past closing time!”

Maxi hesitated before handing me the machine, “Don’t touch any more stones!”

I glared at the stones as I finished scanning them. I was unnerved by what had happened and was starting to get angry with what I couldn’t understand. Maxi kept glancing at me as he worked his way through the henge with his own radar, as if I was a bomb that might go off at any moment. That did nothing to help my mood and I stayed quiet as we finished up and piled back into the van.

The journey back to Avebury was uneventful. I looked for signs of the dead spiders as we drove along, but the clean-up team were long gone. The dry fields rolled past my unseeing eyes as I tried to process the day.

Chapter 10

Madam Mim was waiting at the door as we arrived holding a tray of sweet teas. We each grabbed one and went inside.

Dot was wrapped in a scarlet chunky knitted jumper, lounging on one of the squishy sofas as we entered the cottage. She raised her head from her knitting. It looked like she had moved onto a hat and she gave a cheery wave as if nearly being killed by giant spiders was an everyday part of the job.

I nodded back and trooped upstairs to get washed and changed. Aloora lay on her bed, staring at the slanted ceiling. "Some day huh?"

"Tell me about it! There's a reason I'm an academic!" She looked at me and softened her voice, "It was horrible wasn't it?"

I hugged her tightly to try to reassure her. "Do you want a hot shower or something to eat?"

She gave me an appraising look, "I think you need to wash up first. I'm going to read a bit." She took a long drink of her tea and reached for one of the books on dragons she had bought earlier. Her eyes sparkled as she settled into reading about her favourite topic.

I left her to it and went into our shared bathroom. I stared at the mirror. My hair was normally frizzy but now it was standing straight out from my scalp as if I'd been plugged into static electricity. My face was bright yellow down one side from the tarfangtula blood and the stain continued onto my neck and chest. I grabbed a fluffy folded flannel from a small pile on a wooden shelf and ran it under hot water before scrubbing at the blemish. The effect was to make the skin underneath the yellow stain red and blotchy. Great.

"It's gonna take more than that flannel to get that off love," a gravelly male voice sneered.

I gave a yelp of surprise and looked around the bathroom.

"You wanna try the body scrub in the cabinet. Over here," I finally pinpointed the speaker as the gargoyle perched on the taps of the clawfoot bath.

"Wha?" I said articulately.

The gargoyle sighed, "The cupboard, over there." He nodded his head at the only cabinet in the room and I opened it to find the entire range of Madam Mim's beauty products staring back at me. I sifted through the bottles until I found an amber body scrub promising me "rejuvenation extraordinaire". I held it up to the gargoyle who nodded.

Warily, I tipped some onto the wet flannel and scrubbed hard. When I looked back in the mirror, my face was its usual colour, and looked fresh and healthy. "Wow, thanks er..."

"Gary," the gargoyle supplied. I was expecting a more exotic name but didn't want to be rude.

"Thanks Gary."

"Now it doesn't work on clothes you know…" he said suggestively. I looked down at my top, also stained yellow. There was no way I was getting changed in front of a sentient tap. I hurriedly finished scrubbing until I was satisfied all remnants of spider goo were gone, then I used water to flatten down my hair before going back into the room.

Aloora stood and removed her headphones to go in. "Er, make sure you cover up the tap before you get undressed."

She stared at me as if I was mad and padded into the bathroom. I started to count under my breath. I got to three before I heard her yelp and a muffled laugh from Gary.

I got changed into a cotton tank top and new pair of jeans for dinner. I waited for Aloora to finish up and get dressed.

"So, you still showered then?"

She nodded at me.

"Weren't you worried about…"

"Gary? No, I covered him with a towel. It's fascinating actually, I've never seen a gargoyle so small or one who sits in bathrooms."

Trust Aloora to find a pervert tap fascinating. I rolled my eyes at her and then we went downstairs together.

Dinner was a barbeque outside, taking advantage of the warmth of the summer. Madam Mim's back garden was gorgeous. The borders were built up with rough-hewn stones to make a small wall with a raised flower bed sitting on top of it. Fragrant herbs and delicate flowers were tightly packed so that none of the rich black soil was visible. Glazed pots in bright colours were dotted about the lawn containing heady lavender, rosemary and other plants I didn't know the names of. A path made of cobblestones wound its way through the neat lawn behind a wooden screen which supported climbing roses in every colour of the rainbow.

The old fashioned barbeque sat on a neat patio outside, the smell of charcoal driving Errol crazy as he begged for chunks. Maxi and Lorandir sat on the stone wall and threw him small pieces, trying to encourage him to do tricks, laughing as he soared into the air turning somersaults.

Madam Mim stood at the grill turning burgers and sausages with precision. A wooden patio table, painted duck egg blue, with matching chairs was laden with salads and bread rolls. My mouth watered and I snuck a cherry tomato from one of the bowls. Dot was tucked under a large sun shade, wearing a wide brimmed straw hat.

I smiled, "So the rumours are true."

She gave me a megawatt grin, showing me her fangs, "Well I won't turn to dust straight away, but yes, I am sensitive to the sun," she sighed, "more's the pity."

"You don't like being a vampire?" I helped myself to salad as the others joined us at the table.

Dot shrugged, "It wasn't my choice…I mean there are some perks…but there are also some drawbacks." She moved her hand out from the shade onto a sunny part of the table. It began to turn red. She shook it and move it back in the shadow where it turned back to her usual skin tone. She gave me a sad smile and took a bite of her burger.

She saw me staring, "I enjoy the taste." I was about to question her further when Madam Mim interrupted.

"I understand your day was…eventful?"

Agent Jones glared at her, “That’s one way to describe the attack. What I want to know is who knew we were coming and why they were trying to stop us.”

Madam Mim smiled enigmatically, “What do the readings show?”

“The initial readings are very exciting!” Maxi leaned forwards and grabbed another hot dog, “This could confirm our theories! I’ll analyse the rest of the data tonight!”

“I want to see the analysis as soon as you’re finished,” Agent Jones grumbled.

We spent the rest of the meal in chit chat, enjoying the sun.

“Do the rest of you have, er, gargoyles in your bathrooms?” Everyone stared at me.

“You mean Gary? He’s one of a kind,” Madam Mim answered in between delicate bites of lettuce.

“Why’s he in our bathroom?”

“Cursed.”

I stared at Mim.

“Interesting, what’s the curse?” Trust Aloora to be more interested in the particulars of curses rather than the fact that we had a pervert creature in our bathroom.

“He upset a powerful fae. I agreed he could shelter here for two hundred years until he’s served his time in exile from his own kind.”

“So you put him in the bathroom?!” I still couldn’t get over this.

“It’s where he chose to be. He moves around occasionally but he likes the clawed feet on the bathtub, I think they remind him of happier times.”

"How does that work?"

"I don't like to question him too much, we live our own lives here."

I was still confused but it looked like Madam Mim was done talking about Gary. She served up fluffy scones instead. Maxi and Aloora nearly fell out over the correct order to put cream and jam on the baked goods. I decided to stir them both up and deliberately swirled mine together into a delicious mess before cramming it into my mouth with a wink. They stared at me in horror and began a discussion on the origins of cream teas. I just enjoyed eating the things.

The sun was just beginning to set when Maxi and Agent Jones headed in to complete the analysis of the readings. They set themselves up at the kitchen table with glasses of tonic water and were soon looking at spreadsheets filled with data.

Dot stayed in the garden, wrapping a home-made shawl around her shoulders even though the night was still warm. I decided to head to bed, my muscles were aching from their earlier exertions and my head was still swirling from whatever had happened at Stonehenge.

I woke up in the night in a cold sweat. Aloora was screaming in her bed. I reached over to shake her shoulder and fell out of bed. Cursing, I managed to reach her and shook her awake. Her eyes widened in horror before she focused on me and sighed.

"Oh god, they were everywhere."

"It's ok, there's no one here," I tried to comfort her, my sleep addled brain struggling to stay awake.

"I keep seeing their pedipalps looming over me." I struggled to keep up with Aloora when fully awake, her landing words like pedipalps on me in the middle of the night was unfair.

"Wha're pedipolyps?"

She stared at me and spelled it out, "Mouth parts."

"Oh right, yeah, they were terrifying."

"Exactly." she shuddered.

I rubbed my eyes, "Hot chocolate?" Aloora nodded and we crept downstairs in our pyjamas. I was thankful I'd remembered to bring a full set and not just relied on an oversized t-shirt like I usually did at home.

As I flicked on the light in the kitchen, my eyes lit on a tray set on the table. It was laden with mugs, hot chocolate powder and marshmallows. Madam Mim's psychic powers had never been more welcome. I mixed up two sturdy earthenware mugs of hot chocolate, slightly surprised and relieved to find a microwave in the old kitchen.

We took our mugs back upstairs and sat in bed, the hot chocolate warming and comforting as I sipped it. Errol curled up next to my friend.

"Hey, remember the time we wanted hot chocolate so badly we used Mum's cocoa and didn't realise you had to add sugar?"

Aloora snorted, "Urg, that was disgusting. I still can't believe how far you spit it out across the kitchen!"

We giggled, "Was this what you imagined our girls' trip would be?"

"No, not really. I guess maybe joining a magical taskforce wasn't the best bonding idea," Aloora looked melancholy as she swirled her drink.

"Hey, nothing like fighting off monsters to bond with your friends!" I reached my mug over to hers and we clinked them together as if we were some sort of warrior Vikings celebrating a good battle.

We were quiet for a few minutes, sorting through our own personal memories of the fight. I started to speak to Aloora and was greeted by soft snores. Typical. I carefully took the mug from her hand and put it on the bedside table before snuggling back under my own floral blanket.

I was just drifting back to sleep when something pinged on the edge of my consciousness. I looked around the room, nothing here. My hand went to my axe on the floor between our beds, then I stopped and concentrated. The tugging on my consciousness was from one of the traps at my shop. Something had set it off. I closed my eyes and reached through my connection with the trap to try to see more. I had a vague impression of that strange twisted elven magic again and then my head pounded as the connection abruptly ended.

I rubbed my temples quietly and grabbed my phone to text Marco.

Careful going into the shop. I think one of the traps pinged. Call me if you need help. x

No reply. I checked the phone's clock. 5am. No sane person was up at that hour. I considered calling the police but as I played through the conversation that a magical trap had woken me up over one hundred miles away, it didn't sound believable even to me.

I lay down and tried to will myself back to sleep, breathing in and out rhythmically. After five breaths I gave up, grabbed my mug and shuffled back downstairs.

This time I made a coffee and hot chocolate mix, in an effort both to get rid of the oncoming headache and wake myself up properly. I stepped into the garden onto a dewy lawn and decided to follow the path past the rose trellis into the hidden part of the garden. I made a game of hopping from one paving slab to another up to the wooden frame. I paused to take in the heady scent of the coloured roses and then passed through into a fairy world.

The rough-hewn stone wall morphed into greyish blue flints and built up into three tiers at the back of the garden. A soft waterfall trickled down the flints into a mossy pool dug into the lawn. Somehow, there were ancient trees around this part of the garden, as if it were a cultivated glade in a forest. The sunlight began to twinkle through the branches, soft beams of light hitting on a mossy floor. I sensed magic over the forest, it felt wild yet somehow contained. I wished I had brought my goggles with me and made a mental note to keep them on me for the rest of the mission. A carved marble bench next to the water looked like the perfect place to sit and stop my head reeling in amazement.

The marble was warm despite the cool morning air. I looked around the garden half expecting to see fairies flitting between the flowers. An exotic bird sang a lilting melody as it flitted through the branches of the tall trees, a flash of red and gold against the greenery. I closed my eyes, inhaling the soft scents of moss, water, rich soil and fragrant blossoms.

“Beautiful isn’t it?” a familiar male voice interrupted my peace. I opened my eyes and nodded dumbly. I was acutely aware of being in my pyjamas while he was fully dressed in a tight fitting t-shirt and jeans. I made to stand.

Lorandir sighed, “No, don’t go, I’ll leave.”

He sounded lonely and vulnerable, so different from the cocky elf I thought I knew. Before I could think things through, my treacherous mouth blurted out, “Stay, there’s space on the bench.”

He gave me a surprisingly shy smile and sat next to me. The bench was small but he thoughtfully left some space between us. I had left the charm Gunther had given me against elven glamour in my room, along with Bane, so I was wary. I took a long drink of my coffee chocolate mixture, deliberately staring at the forest. He seemed content to sit quietly so in the end, I broke the silence.

“Madam Mim is certainly not what she seems, is she?”

Lorandir nodded, “Not everyone has access to fae lands.”

My eyes widened and I looked more closely at the forest. “Fae?” I swallowed, the fae were notorious for schemes, tricks and requiring favours in return, but I hadn’t sensed any magical aura from Madam Mim at all.

He laughed good naturedly, “She’s not fae, and it would be Agent Jones obligated for our visit not you.”

“You sound wiser than you look,” I relaxed then realised that could sound like an insult, bit my bottom lip nervously and started to backtrack, “I, er, mean you, erm, look young.” It was a feeble attempt. Fortunately he laughed again, a rich heady laugh that made me want to join in and I remembered why I was suspicious of elven glamour.

“So, how old are you?”

Lorandir turned his green eyes on me and tilted his head to one side, considering me carefully. "I am one hundred years old this year."

"Huh," I took another sip of my drink, trying to do some fuzzy mental arithmetic on how old he would be in human years and then dwarven years. I failed and my puzzling must have shown on my face.

"That's about twenty five in human years."

"Huh," I said again, "so I'm technically older than you." He snorted as if I'd said something really funny and I bristled, standing. "I'd better go get dressed."

He grabbed my free hand as I started to stand and I turned to face him, my eyebrows creasing together.

"I'm sorry." He tugged his fingers through his short hair, messing it up so it fell into a style most pop stars would kill for.

I was genuinely confused now as I started to list possibilities in my head. For laughing at me… For interrupting my morning's peace... For kissing me... For leaving without even saying goodbye... For pretending like it had never happened... I hadn't realised I'd been so upset by that. I decided to make him spell it out, at least I'd know where I stood then, "For what?"

"I should not have…" he looked down at his knees, his usual confidence gone. I almost felt sorry for him but I was annoyed now.

"Kissed me? Look, Lorandir, don't even worry about it. It's in the past, forgotten," I lied.

"It was dishonourable of me to..." I interrupted him with a snort. It was the twenty first century dammit! And if he was so upset about it, why did he even kiss me in the first place. I was about to storm off when he tightened his grip on my hand.

"I am sorry. Every time I'm near you I seem to say or do the wrong things, I don't mean to make you angry, I…enjoy spending time with you." He looked down as if that was a big admission or a guilty secret. I felt a blush starting to make its way up my body and I was annoyed too. I didn't trust my mouth so I kept quiet.

He ran his hand through his hair again, and sighed deeply, "I know trust is earned. Can we start again? Be friends? Can you give me a chance to earn your trust Amethyst?" His green eyes pleaded with mine. I didn't know if it was elven glamour or how he almost purred my name or if I was just soft, but I decided I wanted to get to know him better.

"Fine," I huffed. Well I couldn't let the elf have it all his own way. He smiled widely, looking like I had given him the answer he had hoped for and turned my hand in his so my palm was facing down. Then, with his eyes locked on mine, he bent his head and pressed his lips against the back on my hand. It was the sort of gesture an old fashioned knight might have done for a lady in times of yore.

"Thank you for giving me the chance to earn your trust and your friendship," I think it was the most honest and romantic anyone had ever been with me. I melted. No one had ever kissed my hand or made it sound like my friendship was a treasure to be earned on a quest. Elven cul. I had no idea how to deal with these feelings so I forced them inside me and turned quickly so he couldn't see the blush creeping up my face.

"I really do have to get dressed you know," I scurried off, hearing him stand and follow behind.

Chapter 11

Agent Jones was sitting in the kitchen as we walked through the stable door. She raised an eyebrow at the two of us entering together and took a knowing sip of her black coffee. She was already immaculately dressed in another linen suit. This one was a creamy off-white colour that set off her copper skin. Madam Mim was cooking breakfast in a cast iron saucepan on the stove. A delicious salty smell promised bacon. I looked at the large cat shaped clock in the kitchen. It was ten to six. Was everyone an early riser?

I put my mug in the sink, wincing as the pottery clanged heavily on the ceramic butler sink. Nothing broke and I walked upstairs, pointedly ignoring the agent and the elf.

Aloora was still asleep, her arm curled above her head restfully. Errol had curled up at her feet, snoring softly. I tiptoed to the bathroom to wash up.

"'Ello love, did ya miss me?" Gary the gargoyle stuck his tongue out from his perch on top of the taps.

"I'm not in the mood," I stuffed a large towel over him and made sure it was tucked tightly around him. So far he'd just talked, not moved, but I wasn't taking any chances. I looked longingly at the deep claw foot bath. It was a real shame, I'd have loved a long soak. Instead I had the quickest shower I'd ever had, my back turned pointedly to the grumbling gargoyle.

I got dressed before I woke my friend. She groaned and rolled over, "Five more minutes," she grunted into the pillow.

"Sorry Ally, looks like everyone's an early riser here."

She groaned more loudly and pushed the covers off. Errol landed on the ground with a thump and wandered downstairs to find some bacon. I left her to get ready, knowing my friend was definitely not a morning person and followed the wyrm to the kitchen.

Madam Mim had already set Errol's breakfast in a bowl on the floor and he was slobbering in his enthusiasm to wolf up the food. I sat at the table and helped myself to bacon and eggs with a side of hot buttered toast. I was relieved that I was the only one there and ate in peace.

Aloora stomped in a quarter of an hour later and poured herself a bowl of healthy cereal with fruit and nuts in it. She sat huddled on one side of the table, scrolling on her phone. I knew better than to engage her in conversation so finished my own breakfast before grabbing my jewelling goggles that allowed me to see magical auras and making my way to the living room. Maxi entered the kitchen just as I was leaving. I heard him try to engage my friend in conversation and smiled wryly to myself. Moments later, he came into the lounge, balancing a stack of toast on an earthenware plate.

"Healthy eating, what!" he exclaimed as he sat on the sofa and perched the plate on a side table. I wasn't sure if he was joking or not, but I didn't think six slices of toast lathered in butter and honey was that good for you. I kept my mouth shut though. He didn't seem to mind the silence and munched happily on toast while expounding on the benefits of honey. I tuned out and flipped through one of Aloora's books that she'd left on a comfy chair. It was about the legends of dragons across the British Isles and there were some quite interesting stories in there, as well as some gruesome pictures taken from medieval manuscripts.

Agent Jones and Maxi began poring over a small laptop, pointing between the screen and printouts from a portable printer Maxi had set up. I left them to talk of "magical anomalies" and lost myself in the book about dragons.

"You know, they say that once dragons allowed themselves to be ridden," Lorandir's voice broke my concentration as he pointed towards a picture on the page. Colourful ink captured a dragon in flight, breathing fire at a castle while a smaller armoured rider sat astride it.

"That was a long time ago of course, well before this manuscript was created. In fact, there's tales of dragons living in harmony with many species before they began their long hibernation," Aloora had entered the room and sank into a squashy chair next to mine, now fully awake. "They shared their knowledge with magical beings and the world was better for it, some of the most beautiful pieces were forged with help from dragons." Her eyes turned misty as she thought to that long lost time. I knew she dreamed of a world where dragons coexisted peacefully with other species. My own thoughts turned to the Fang Dagger that I had been threatened with by crazy cultists earlier in the year. I wasn't sure I'd describe it as beautiful…dangerous or terrifying or powerful maybe. I couldn't deny the workmanship though, what would it take to work with a piece of a dragon? I couldn't even imagine creating something so powerful.

"Hey, that rider is wielding an axe like yours Ame," Lorandir pointed eagerly at a picture over my shoulder.

I studied the page. The axe did look a lot like Bane. There wasn't a lot of detail in the picture but the manuscript artist had attempted to illustrate the glow of an enchanted axe in use as the dwarf stood over a pile of bloodied corpses. I read the text underneath the picture out loud, "'Erik Lieffson wielding Bloodbane as he smote his enemies, taken from *The Lieffson Saga*.' That explains it, my family claims Lieffson as an ancestor and our axe was modelled on the original Bloodbane, that's why my axe is called Bane actually."

Agent Jones broke into our conversation, "Right everyone, today we're going to map out the Avebury circle, same as we did yesterday. I want to get this done early before tourists start arriving. Tomorrow is the Summer Solstice so I want this all done well before then. Amethyst, you will be part of the ground team this time," she added meaningfully. I didn't dare roll my eyes and stared off into the mid-distance, feeling my face heat at the reminder of the strange events at Stonehenge.

She took me aside after the short briefing and handed me a leather scabbard. "It was fashioned for a sword, but I cut a hole in the bottom, I reckon it will do for your axe until you get a proper one made."

"Thank you, I…"

She held up a manicured hand, "Don't. I want us all armed, just in case."

I pushed away my curiosity about where she had found a scabbard, she probably wouldn't tell me anyway. "Where's Dot?"

"She's sleeping," Agent Jones gave me a look as if I was stupid and I felt the blush creep over my face again. "She's a vampire, you know, nocturnal. She did us a massive favour yesterday but I've given her today off to catch up on her sleep."

She strapped her crossbow in a holster on her thigh and strode out of the door. We followed, all carrying our own weapons. Even Aloora had one of the daggers I'd made strapped around her waist. I had no idea how Agent Jones had managed to get scabbards for everything. I paused to hurriedly rub in some suncream, it seemed as if everyone else was lucky enough to tan and not burn in the summer sun. Madam Mim smiled knowingly at us as we went, slowly stirring her own cup of tea.

We walked the short distance to the stone circle. I called Marco on the way to let him know to be careful at the shop, just in case. He sounded excitable on the phone and was apparently already at the shop and hadn't seen any signs of intruders. That made me more nervous. How good were they that they hadn't left any signs? He brushed off my concern and hung up after assurances that he would be careful and that the design work was going great. I wasn't sure how that made me feel, but I was glad he was ok.

As we entered one of the fields containing the stone circle, Maxi handed me a large ground penetrating radar and flipped it on for me. Agent Jones lined us up and we set out, slowly scanning the ground.

I had given up on wearing my goggles when I realised they weren't helping me see much. The rocks had a dull red aura to them, and I guessed dwarves had carved them and infused them with magic. The glass also stopped me reading the radar properly and had started to give me a headache. The screen glowed with technicolour lines as I paced up and down the field in my assigned quadrant. I had no idea what it meant, but judging by Maxi's excitement yesterday, it probably confirmed the theory that there was a magical energy signature around here.

I sweated in my high neck tank top, jeans and gothic boots as I walked in the morning sun. Even the amethyst in my pocket felt hot through my jeans. Errol stayed near me today, uncharacteristically nervous, he trotted so close to my feet he nearly tripped me up twice. I reached down to try to reassure him and got a nip on the hand for my trouble. He was anxious about something.

I was in the southern part of the circle and noticed the pattern on the screen narrowing as I went further south. It continued off the field and I followed it as far as I could until a wire fence stopped me.

"Haernson! What are you doing? Get back to your position!" Agent Jones shouted across the field at me. I must be in trouble if she was last naming me. I turned back and stuck to the original instructions.

We were done by lunchtime, despite covering a larger area than Stonehenge spread all around the town, and Maxi and Agent Jones took the radar devices back to Madam Mim's house to analyse the data.

"Pub?" I suggested to Aloora, who nodded. Lorandir tagged along too. We sat outside at a picnic bench shaded by a sun umbrella. The heat had turned heavy and sticky as if a thunderstorm was brewing and I brushed the sweat from my face. I'd have loved to sit inside the pub's cool interior, but guessed as they didn't welcome dogs inside, a pet wyrm wouldn't be welcome either. Errol loved heat of any kind and now we were away from the stone circle, he sprawled out on the dry grass, sun bathing. I envied him sometimes.

"What do you think?" Aloora asked eagerly once we had got our drinks. Vodka and coke for me, a bitter shandy for Aloora and mead for Lorandir.

I perused the menu, "Fish and chips. Easy choice."

"Not about the food," she rolled her eyes, "about the magical signature?"

I blinked at her.

"It's big for sure," Lorandir answered her, sipping his mead slowly.

"I'm not certain what all the lines and colours meant, but it looked like it headed south." I added, feeling left out.

"Interesting, I thought the same when I was scanning yesterday, that the energy seemed to expand beyond Stonehenge. North though." Aloora mused.

"They couldn't be connected could they?"

"Don't see why not. We don't even know for sure why these circles were built and these two are so close to each other, they could be related."

My stomach rumbled loudly. Lorandir had the grace to take another sip to cover his laugh. I started to glare at him then remembered we were meant to be trying to get along so decided to ignore him instead.

"All I know for sure is that walking around all morning has made me hungry!" I picked up the menu, asked what they wanted and went inside to place our orders.

It annoyed me a little to find them talking about dragons and henges when I went back outside. I drank in silence as I wondered why I was annoyed. Was I jealous that they could talk civilly to each other whereas I always seemed to be snapping at Lorandir? Or did I feel like a third wheel as they were clearly getting along and had similar interests?

I was glad for the distraction of the food arriving and tucked in vigorously. Errol stirred from his sun bathing to hoover up any titbits that fell under the table. We relaxed as we ate and the conversation turned away from musing over our mission.

"My round next, what shall we have? Shots?" Lorandir joked.

"No way, the last time Ame had shots, she ended up in A&E!"

I groaned, "Thanks for bringing that up!"

The elf sat back down, "I need to hear that story."

I put my head in my hands, plotting my revenge as Aloora carried on. "Well, we were at a bar in Cardiff and they had two for one on these sweet flavoured shots. We decided to try them all – rhubarb and custard, chocolate limes, liquorice…"

"Ugh, the liquorice one!" I gagged at the thought of that particular flavour.

"They had these waiters going round with little white hats on and aprons like they were old fashioned sweet shop owners. Anyway, after round six, lemon sherbet if I recall correctly, Ame grabbed a hat and tray off one of these waiters and climbed up onto a table. She started dancing around, spilling drinks everywhere! People were crowding round with their mouths open to catch the shots as Ame poured them while she twirled. The staff couldn't decide whether to stop her or not, they were so busy laughing!

"Well, the table got so slippery with all these drinks going everywhere that she fell off. And not one of those people crowding round caught her. The staff stopped laughing at that, especially when she started shouting that she couldn't walk! After a trip to A&E, not fun on a Friday night, and one twisted ankle later, Ame's sworn off shots!"

We were all laughing at that, Lorandir even snorted. I decided I liked it when his elven veneer of perfection fell.

"Oh yeah, well what about the time you decided you were dating the statue of Aneurin Bevan?!" I said with a wicked smile at my friend.

Her face turned to mock horror, "We swore never to speak of that!"

"Fair's fair! Ally here had just gone through a rough break up after her girlfriend at the time, Lilith I think it was, plagiarised one of her assignments…"

"Academic work should be sacred!"

I put my hand on her arm, "No one's arguing. She was a total cul. Anyway, so we decided to call off our Dungeons and Dragons session and go drinking so Ally could get over her. We had sooo many cocktails and were staggering home through the city centre when this statue caught her eye. She climbed up…"

"To take the traffic cone off of his head, I was doing a public service," Aloora chimed in weakly.

"Yeah yeah. So she gets the traffic cone off, almost falls then starts proclaiming that the statue saved her and was the only trustworthy thing worth dating in the whole of Wales! I think you even snogged it!"

It was her turn to groan now. I laughed and turned to Lorandir, "OK, you've heard our most embarrassing stories, your turn elf boy."

"Hmmm," he tapped his chin, "well the thing about elves is we have longer lives than many other beings, so our teenage years last longer too, which means I have more embarrassing stories than I care to remember. But I think one of the most embarrassing things happened when I was about eighteen in human years at home in Breconia.

"I had drunk a bit too much fermented wine at lunchtime with my cousins and we decided to climb trees and show off in the forest. So we started climbing these trees and then doing backflips on the branches, seeing who could jump the highest…who could balance on the narrowest branch, that sort of thing.

"I was winning the competition when I mistimed a somersault completely. I ended up falling, hitting a lot of branches on the way down, but that wasn't the worst part. Somehow my belt snagged on a branch about head height from the ground. So there I was dangling from this tree, bruised from my fall and all my friends laughing at me when I hear someone coming.

"I start shouting up for help but it's too late. The Elfish King and Queen walk into view complete with their full court retinue. Everyone stops and stares at me. I can't do anything. Then the branch breaks and I crash to the ground in front of the whole royal court. The captain of the guards runs over and takes me into custody to cool off and sober up. My friends have never let me forget it."

“That was only ‘one of’ your embarrassing stories?” Aloora said as I held my side laughing at the dignified elf hanging from a tree. I definitely preferred this slightly goofy Lorandir.

“I want to hear them all!” I leaned forward. We spent another hour sharing stories before heading back to the cottage companionably.

Chapter 12

Madam Mim ushered us in before Lorandir had the chance to ring the doorbell. I was beginning to wonder if it was just there for show.

I heard raised voices coming from the living room.

"This was a fact finding mission only!" Agent Jones's voice was unmistakeable.

Madam Mim pointed us through the kitchen to the garden. She joined us a few minutes later with earthenware mugs of tea for us all. Mine was strong yet milky, just how I liked it. I wondered fleetingly how she knew, one of many questions I had concerning Madam Mim.

The shouting stopped momentarily and I breathed a sigh of a relief. I couldn't imagine Maxi yelling at anyone. The relief was short lived. Agent Jones' voice blared loudly. The words were muffled but the tone gave me a sense of frustration.

Dot walked out, yawning and carrying a glass of something red. I hoped it was cranberry juice but didn't want to ask. She was wearing another chunky jumper, hugging one arm around her midriff as if she was cold. I nodded to her.

"Can't sleep?"

She shook her head, "Not with that racket going on. I've never heard Ruth so angry."

"Ruth?"

"Special Agent Jones." I had forgotten she had a first name, Agent seemed to fit her so well.

"What's she yelling about?"

Both Dot and Lorandir cocked their heads. With their supernatural hearing, I was sure they could make out every word.

"She's talking to her superior on the phone about the findings. He's asked her to do something. She's not happy."

"That's it?"

"Well, that's the gist of it. I mean, there are a few swear words in there and some data readings." Dot shrugged. "If we need to know, we'll find out soon enough. I'm guessing it's about our mission. In my life, I've learned to savour the times when you can just smell the roses." With that, she literally walked over to the climbing roses and sniffed one, closing her eyes and smiling softly.

"How old do you think she is?" Aloora muttered, staring at the vampire.

Dot heard her and looked up with a smile, "Old enough to know better." She winked and walked slowly around the garden, enjoying the fragrant flowers.

"I like her," Aloora walked over to join Dot.

I took the opportunity to stand next to Madam Mim. "So, er, what's with the garden?"

She blinked at me, "Well I use a lot of the herbs in my lotions, potions and tinctures…"

"I mean the magical bit behind the roses."

"Ah, well I always like to have access to my true home, Avalon."

"So you're a, er, fae or something then?" Sometimes I wasn't tactful. I could see Lorandir shaking his head softly out of the corner of my eye.

Madam Mim smiled her knowing smile, "Something like that, yes."

I wanted to press further but Agent Jones stepped out of the patio doors that led onto the living room. She inhaled deeply and pinched the bridge of her nose before glaring around the garden.

"Everybody inside. I'll give you five minutes to refill your drinks. We've got a new mission." She did an abrupt about turn and marched back into the living room.

It wasn't entirely unexpected but we all looked at each other anyway. I headed for the kitchen to boil the kettle. If Agent Jones was as unhappy as she sounded, this wasn't going to be pleasant and I might as well have a drink in my hand.

Everyone seemed to have a similar idea and, with refills in hand, we trooped into the living room. Aloora and I curled up on the squashy sofa. Lorandir lounged on a hardback chair brought from the dining room. Only an elf could make himself comfortable anywhere. Dot settled into one of the cosy armchairs and knitting appeared in her hands from somewhere. Madam Mim leaned against the wall near the door, cup and saucer in her hands.

Maxi was sitting in a chintzy armchair behind Agent Jones, sending her worried glances behind her back as he fiddled with a laptop. Agent Jones was standing in front of the low coffee table. Stacks of paper littered the table, covered with numbers I didn't understand.

"Right, good news is that our mission was a success. We have managed to map both Stonehenge and Avebury stone circles comprehensively, so well done everyone." She met each of our gazes in acknowledgement before carrying on.

"Maxi and I have analysed the data and it's conclusive. There is a definite magical signature beneath the circles. Maxi." Agent Jones stepped to the side and Maxi stood, turning the laptop so we could see the screen. It was a map of the two sites overlaid with radar readings. Swirling reddish oranges, purples and golds streaked across the map.

"Yah so, these colours represent strong magical auras or energies beneath the ground! It is our best guess that the stones were built over some sort of magical concentration! We think this may be either to contain or to mark where dragons are slumbering!" Despite his typical enthusiasm, I thought he looked a little sheepish. He spoke quickly then sat down.

Agent Jones moved forward, commanding the room. "So, my superiors, the 'powers that be'," she didn't try to hide the sarcasm, "have decided in their wisdom that the second part of this mission is to open dialogue with the creatures."

Madam Mim narrowed her eyes. Audible gasps came from the rest of us, apart from Maxi who now looked miserable. Dot even stopped knitting, her needles poised in her hands.

"Alright, alright," Agent Jones raised her hands, "it's not exactly what I want either, but orders are orders. Now you are all part of the taskforce, so technically you are in the employ of the Magical Liaison Office. However, I don't believe in forcing my team into things. So, if you'd rather not be involved in this final part of the mission then you can stay here."

Again, her gaze moved around the room, locking eyes with each of us. Aloora was nodding frantically. Communicating with a dragon was basically Christmas come early for her.

Dot had her head on one side, staring at Agent Jones. "You know me, I'm seeing this through." She shrugged and went back to her knitting.

I knew I had paled. I glanced over at Lorandir. His lounging looked a lot tenser. He met my eyes. We were the only two who had seen a dragon close up. It was the single most terrifying thing I had ever experienced and I still had night terrors about it months later. But I wasn't about to let my best friend do something stupid without me. I knew what I would choose to do.

I nodded tersely, my jaw clenched together. Lorandir faced Agent Jones and nodded too. Schiztz. I had a bad feeling about this.

Agent Jones looked at us, her face still grim. "Thank you, I appreciate your loyalty to the team. Now I want to reassure you that we are communicating only, using radios attuned to draconic brainwaves. Maxi."

He stood once again, "Yah, well, I've been working on these devices, what, and we've tested them on a number of sleeping supernatural beings. We've been able to communicate with them in their dreams and get responses, with none of them waking!"

Aloora raised her hand. I noticed it was shaking slightly with excitement, "How have you defined draconic brainwaves? I assume you don't have a dragon in your laboratory." Great question, I thought.

"Yah, well, that's quite interesting, what! You see we've tested the machines on wyrms as a close proxy for dragon physiology! Even better, with the dragon now awake in Cardiff, we've been able to monitor it using sensors near its nest in the Millennium Stadium!"

I knew Aloora was itching for the technical details of that, but I had to know, "How can you communicate with someone while they're asleep? Aren't they, well, asleep?"

"Excellent question, what! You see, the devices access brainwaves in the subconscious, allowing us to hold a conversation without waking the person up! It's a little like lucid dreaming for the participant!"

I squirmed a little. I didn't like the thought of someone tapping directly into my subconscious. It was creepy enough getting read by Madam Mim. It seemed we were brushing past that ethical quandary though.

Agent Jones stepped forward again, "Right, thank you Maxi, you can get into technical details with anyone who wants them after this briefing is over. Now the even better news is that to maximise success we are going to be attempting contact as soon after the midsummer solstice sunrise as possible."

She huffed out a sigh, "Yes, that is tomorrow morning. Yes, the place will be crawling with civilians, which is why we will be getting there well before sunrise and I have called in some favours to help get the partygoers out of there after sunrise for an hour. That is our window, the boundaries between realms will be thinnest and we are only doing this once. Is that clear?"

We nodded. There wasn't really another option.

"Right, you're off duty for the rest of the day and I suggest you get an early night. We will be leaving two hours before sunrise."

I yawned compulsively at the thought of being up that early. Agent Jones turned back to the screen, arms folded. Maxi looked sheepish. Aloora strode over to get more details about the scans. I decided to go for a walk.

There were a lot more cars around today as the influx of Solstice participants arrived in anticipation of tomorrow. One driver swore at another as a parking spot was taken near the village shop. Other cars had parked up on the kerb rather than find a designated spot. I overheard a couple whinging about the Solstice tourists taking over the small town. I left them to it and hurried back to the cottage. Although I was used to the busy streets of Cardiff, the town felt too crowded. Dark clouds began to gather overhead, intensifying the muggy summer heat.

Chapter 13

My alarm sounded ridiculously early and I blinked blearily as I shrugged off the covers and got up. I had slept poorly. A summer storm had rumbled in the night, chasing away the sticky heat in flashes of lightning and thunder. Errol grumbled too, snorting a smoke ring at me as I nudged him.

"You can sleep in the van boy." I yawned and flipped the lamp on. Aloora groaned and pulled the covers over her head.

"Five more minutes!"

I grabbed a t-shirt and jeans. As I struggled to even get one leg in, I swore that I would go on that diet, get more exercise, and lose those extra pounds that seemed to have crept on. Then I realised I was trying to pull on a pair of Aloora's trousers. I sighed in relief, no wonder I couldn't get into the petite gnome's jeans. I found my own clothes and grabbed my new leather jacket. Although it was midsummer, the night air carried a slight chill after the storm.

I made sure Aloora was getting up before making my way to the stairs, carrying Bane and trying to pull my goggles over my head with my other hand. Errol raced down the steps, his nose high as he smelled the welcome scent of bacon wafting through the cottage. I stumbled as he ran between my legs and let out an involuntary cry as I missed my step and began to fall down the stairs.

I felt a strong hand grab me mid fall and yank me backwards. Too hard. I fell back and collided with my saviour. I turned to see Lorandir rubbing his head where it had connected with the hard wooden bannister.

"Erm, thanks. And sorry about your head," I was rewarded with a grin. I always felt inadequate when confronted with elven beauty. I mean, elves are tall, slender, and gorgeous and I'm five foot nothing and curvaceous. I instinctively checked to make sure the charm Gunther had given me to forestall the effects of elven glamour was in my pocket. It was there, alongside the amethyst I was now carrying like a talisman.

"Don't even worry about it," he echoed one of my favourite sayings. I smiled back. "After you, m'lady."

"No, no, after you, m'gentleman," I joked. A reminder of our time together earlier in the year, when we had slain a monster together and witnessed a dragon awakening…and kissed. Schiztz. He sensed the loss of my sense of humour even though I had carefully kept the smile on my face.

He sighed. Something like disappointment flickered across his face before it settled into his more natural aloof expression,

"Breakfast?" I nodded and we walked into the kitchen in silence. I felt like I was messing everything up.

Maxi was already in the hallway checking the communication equipment and placing each monitor into his backpack once he was satisfied. I said good morning as we passed and he waved distractedly.

Dot was already in the kitchen, grinning and sipping from a mug of something warm. I supposed this was just late at night for her.

I moodily grabbed a bacon roll and dolloped on a large helping of ketchup before stuffing it into my mouth. I couldn't say the wrong thing if I was eating. Madam Mim pushed a large mug of syrupy coffee in my direction and I smiled weakly. It tasted almost as good as my favourite brew from the Dragon's Head back in Cardiff.

Aloora already had her earphones in as she came downstairs last. She waved away breakfast and instead grabbed a coffee in silence. Agent Jones appeared in the doorway and grunted approval as she saw we were all awake.

"Ten minutes," she barked as she grabbed her own coffee and an apple then left.

Madam Mim smiled as if there was some joke we were missing and began packing bacon rolls and fruit into a small satchel that she then slung over her shoulder. It sat oddly against her Victorian style dress.

Exactly ten minutes later, Agent Jones returned and told us to "Move it." A large gibbous moon illuminated the path outside the cottage, casting strange shadows amongst the potted plants that littered the garden.

"It is a night for magic," Madam Mim's soft voice came from behind me, making me jump. She smiled as she swayed up the path to the van and squeezed into the front seat next to Agent Jones. Maxi was compulsively checking the equipment as we set off.

"You're coming with us?" I asked.

She nodded back, her mysterious smile playing over her face, "I never miss the Solstice."

I heard Agent Jones swear as she navigated the narrow road that was Avebury's main street and was now packed with cars. I thought I saw a human-sized winged beast flit over us in the moonlight. More people gathering for the Summer Solstice at this stone circle.

I closed my eyes and dozed, Errol warming my lap in the chill night air.

As we approached Stonehenge, more cars lined the roads. Agent Jones swore again as she braked hard to avoid pedestrians with glow sticks crossing the road. I blinked awake from my light sleep in time to see them moving towards the henge, wobbly neon colours lighting their way.

"Right, I'm going to park then we're moving in. I've arranged to meet my contacts at the entrance. There will be thousands of people there so we need to stick together."

She bumped the van up a grassy verge and got out, slamming the door. "Got everything?"

I tapped Bane, nestled in its temporary scabbard around my waist and lifted Errol onto my shoulder. For the first time I wondered if it had been a mistake to bring him with us. As if sensing my thoughts, Madam Mim handed me a lead.

“Thank you, where…?” I started to ask as I clipped it onto the wyrm’s collar. She smiled and moved off to fall into step behind Agent Jones.

They set a brisk pace despite the darkness and eerie shadows cast by the low moon, and I was glad I had inherited some of Dad’s dwarven night vision. I couldn’t see as well in the dark as a full-blooded dwarf of course, but in the moonlight, it was enough.

We passed a couple of other small groups on the way, buzzing with anticipation. We made it to the main field containing the stones thanks to Agent Jones flashing her badge at the English Heritage stewards on duty. I thought I recognised Roger frowning as we passed through.

The space around the stones was teeming with people. There must have been thousands all crammed into the field. More neon glow sticks sparkled in technicolour flashes from pockets around us. Other, more magical, lighting glowed as well. Festive orbs floated above the crowd and illuminated happy waiting faces.

I had never been to a Summer Solstice festival at Stonehenge before. It was a lot to take in. The air pulsed with magical auras from hundreds upon hundreds of beings crammed into one space. I felt my stomach tighten. The atmosphere and pulsing lights reminded me of a rave. The soundtrack was a lot different to anything I’d experienced in Cardiff nightclubs though.

There were druids robed in white with wreaths upon their heads chanting rhythmically. A group of people were singing out of tune nearby.

"Trying to resonate with the stones," Aloora murmured by my ear as she stared at the crowds, as overwhelmed as I was by the sheer number of people.

I saw nimble figures outlined in grey pre-dawn light as they leapt across the horizontal lintel stones in feats of acrobatics. Elves.

I was elbowed out of the way by a group of dwarves dressed in rainbow coloured clothing as they deployed pointy elbows, knees and hobnailed boots to push their way closer to the stones themselves. I was glad I was wearing my own heavy duty boots as one of them trod on my foot as they passed.

I pulled my goggles over my eyes, immediately able to see all the magical auras I had sensed. The kaleidoscope of colours was beautiful and overpowering. Auras of every colour lit up the area. It looked as if the stones themselves were glowing too, a combination of red and gold, although there were so many people pressed up to the henge, it could have been the build-up of power. So much magical energy started to give me a headache and I lifted my jewelling goggles.

Aloora nudged me sharply in the stomach, pulling my attention away from the revelries to where Agent Jones was talking to a tall man and, yes, that was Roger. We forced our way through the throngs of people until we were close enough to hear what they were saying.

"…you've got to be joking!"

"I wish I was, Roger, but those are my orders. We won't interfere with the sunrise itself of course. We'll set up around the perimeter and as soon as the sun is fully over the horizon, we need everyone to leave."

"There's eight thousand people here! You do know that?"

"Then it's a good job we're prepared," she tapped Maxi's backpack and gestured to some large black boxes on the floor next to the tall man. She softened her voice, "I understand, OK, it's not what I would have chosen either, but it's what we have to do and I'd rather you helped than I called in more back up. All I'm asking is that you tell people they have to leave straight after the sunrise, you can do that can't you?"

Roger crossed his arms tightly, clearly unhappy, "I want to speak to your superiors."

Agent Jones held out her phone, "If you want to call my boss before four in the morning, go ahead."

He shifted uncomfortably, "Fine! I'll do it, but don't blame me when no one leaves. This is the largest Solstice event in Britain and it's important to all of them."

Agent Jones smiled, "Thank you." She turned, effectively dismissing Roger and took a pace towards the taller man. I felt sorry for the steward as he grumbled and returned to his post muttering about the "Bloody Magical Liaison Office."

"All set?"

The tall man nodded. A magical orb floated overhead as it followed a pair of wizards ambling towards the henge. I could see his heavy set features illuminated by their orb and felt the power flowing from him. A sorcerer.

"Just need some help getting these into place," he gestured to the black boxes and I shone my phone's torch over at them. Speakers. I frowned.

"What are they for?"

Agent Jones turned and gave me a look, "They're to help us clear these people out in exactly," she glanced at her watch, "one hour's time. Not even I can shout loudly enough to be heard over that racket."

"Was that a joke?" I whispered to myself as Agent Jones turned back to the sorcerer.

"I think so," Lorandir's reply came from close behind me. Bloody elven hearing. "If Agent Jones is making jokes, it must mean the world's about to end. It was nice knowing you." His voice was tight behind the joking words.

I gave him an appraising look and noticed his features looked drawn and uncomfortable. He was nervous. I felt the knot that had grown in my stomach loosen a little.

I patted his arm familiarly and smiled, "Nice knowing you too."

"Alright you two love birds, get helping. We need to get these speakers up across the field. Maxi will show you where." Agent Jones broke into the moment, before she grabbed one end of a large speaker and lifted it with the sorcerer.

Dot and Aloora picked up another one and made to follow them. I walked up to the third one and grabbed an end. Lorandir gripped the other and we lifted it. It wasn't too heavy but it tilted at a crazy angle as I'm five foot nothing and he was over six foot tall.

We swayed our way along past groups of friends readying themselves for the solstice. Some had their phones out and were live streaming on social media. An elderly man was taking pictures with a large lensed camera. I turned to look at an odd noise coming from one group of goblins then quickly looked away, almost tripping over my own feet in shock. I wasn't one hundred per cent sure what they were doing but I did not want any insights into a possible goblin orgy.

We followed behind Maxi until he nodded to indicate we should put it down. He immediately bent down and began fiddling with the connections. I asked how it could work when it wasn't connected to a power source and he gave me a look.

"Magic!" Of course. That explained the sorcerer.

He finished and rushed after the others to check their speakers. I looked around. The greyish pre-dawn light was beginning to colour. Sunrise was drawing closer. Errol sniffed at the ground, darting around and straining against his lead as he picked up scents of animals long gone.

Our speaker was positioned to the left of the circle. Most of the people here to celebrate the solstice had placed themselves within the stones, facing eastwards, waiting for sunrise. The sky began to lighten from grey to a soft pastel pink. The storm had left raindrops sprinkled on the ground that mingled with the morning dew and magical energy to give everything a sparkle. It was as if the whole place was covered in fairy dust. The light began to intensify, picking out a wisp of cloud in a surreal pink. I almost took out my phone to snap a picture for Marco but that seemed like it would dishonour the moment somehow.

An expectant hush fell over the crowd. The absence of noise somehow loud as anticipation thrummed across the field. Humans and magical beings alike joined in appreciation of this time-honoured event.

The sun crested over the horizon in a blaze of orange. The crowd cheered as one. I felt myself smiling, caught up in the enthusiasm. It was only a sunrise and yet it was more than that, a symbol of hope, of renewal. I felt free somehow of a weight I hadn't known I was carrying.

The sun continued to rise slowly, slowly. Its rays reached across the dew-laden grass towards the stones and illuminated them. A small contingent of the crowd had begun an impromptu dance, swaying and holding up long skirts as they twirled.

I felt a rumble come through the speaker. I frowned as it glowed slightly. The sorcerer must have started his magic. Surely Agent Jones was waiting for the full sunrise, for the glowing orb to completely crest the horizon before she put a halt to this celebration. I tried to find her through the multitude of people but it was no use.

The speaker continued to emit a low rumbling. I couldn't make out any words but a few people were starting to look our way, annoyed at the interruption to their festivities.

I met Lorandir's eyes and he shrugged. I crossed my arms, unwilling to ask people to move. We hadn't been given any orders to interfere so I just stood there, unable to enjoy the remainder of the sunrise. Errol stopped sniffing the ground and began to move more agitatedly around. I reached down to stroke his head and soothe him, but he backed away from me and tried to pull away, straining on the lead.

As we waited, the rumbling intensified. It seemed as if the entire ground was shaking. How loud was this speaker? I bent down to try to find a volume control, it didn't seem right to keep it blaring out incoherent sounds, I could at least turn it down until Agent Jones started speaking.

As I knelt by the device, it felt that the ground was vibrating even more violently. "What the dzrak?" I mumbled to myself as I pressed my hand to the damp grass.

I didn't think this was part of the plan. I pressed my ear to the ground, as if that would help me at all. I wasn't a tracker in some film. To my surprise, I heard the rumbling from the speaker stop and another, deeper noise reply. From underground.

Schiztz. I gestured to Lorandir to join me and after a strange look, he lay on the ground next to me, his hands pressed to the ground either side of his head as he listened. His elven hearing was far superior to mine and his expression quickly changed from one that indicated I was crazy to anxious. It was only when he made to get up that I realised I was holding his hand. Schiztz.

I got to my feet with a burst of embarrassed speed, "Well, what was that?"

Lorandir shook his head, "Nothing good. It sounded like something was replying to the sounds from the speaker…the only time I've heard anything close to that was…" he swallowed and I finished the sentence for him.

"…when the dragon woke up?"

He nodded. Errol scrambled up my body, digging his claws through my clothes as he tried to get away from the ground.

"We need to warn the others!" I stated the obvious. I started waving to try to attract some attention but only succeeded in starting a Mexican wave across the field.

I huffed in frustration and took out my phone, frantically trying to dial Aloora's number. She didn't pick up. Schiztz. I checked my display. No signal. The magical energy from the crowd must be blocking the networks.

I stepped away from the henge, waving my phone around as I tried to get a signal. Lorandir was doing the same. I heard a shout of triumph and raced towards him.

"No! I've got signal, don't come close and use it up with your phone! It's ringing!" He practically shouted at me. I knew he was really worried then, I didn't think I'd ever seen so much emotion from the elf.

I heard Agent Jones answer gruffly but not her words as Lorandir explained what we'd felt and heard. He gazed at the phone. "She hung up!"

Some of the revellers had started to notice the shaking now and were looking around nervously wondering if it was part of the ceremonial power or something else.

Chapter 14

A shout of protest sounded from the mass of people gathered to celebrate the Solstice. I squinted over the crowd. More yelling. It sounded closer this time. "Watch where you're going!"

I saw movement in the crowd. Someone was pushing through, heading towards us. I reached for my trusty axe at the same time as the figure made its way to the edge of the crowd. A blast of power hit me hard in the chest and I went flying backwards. I felt heat rise from the amethyst gem in my back pocket at the impact. Errol leapt from my shoulder as I fell, giving a bark of annoyance as he landed on all fours. I wasn't as graceful. I landed hard on my tailbone with an involuntary shout of pain. There was a dull heat where the shot of magic had hit my chest, but I was unharmed. Odd. That much energy should have fried me.

I heard Lorandir yell “Sheld!” as he activated the shield rune I had engraved on his sword. I didn’t have time to dwell on why I wasn’t more hurt. I had to help. I heaved myself upwards and moved close to him to get within the protective barrier, drawing Bane as I went. My other hand gripped Errol’s lead tightly to make sure he was safe and close by. The figure raised a hand towards us and loosed another blast of power. The shield held and fiery red magic crackled where it connected with the invisible barrier. I took a moment to have a craftswoman’s pride in the weapon I’d created.

The figure was joined by two more, dressed identically in dark robes. The rising sun lit them, showing clearly the familiar dark red colour of the cloaks. Schiztz. The same colour that the cult had worn when they had awakened the dragon under Cardiff Castle.

I didn’t like where this was leading. If they were here, it looked like Maxi’s analysis had been right and there really was a dragon underneath Stonehenge and these idiots were trying to wake that one from its thousands of years of slumber too.

With these unhappy thoughts swirling round my head, Lorandir had to shout to pull my attention back to the fight.

“Hey! Get your head in the game!” he snapped. I nodded and gripped Bane more firmly. The shield would only last for a small amount of time. The cultists were moving towards us, the middle one keeping up a steady barrage of magical blasts on the shield.

The others had drawn weapons. Cruel serrated blades glinted in the morning sun. As they approached, I stepped out of the protective shield and swung hard. The figure blocked, with more strength than I was expecting and I twisted the axe in my grip so it slid down the blade. The weapon didn't have a large hilt and Bane sliced through it and into the hand gripping the knife. I was rewarded with a cry of pain and the cultist fell to the ground, clutching its hand.

I ran back into the shield's force field as the magic user sent a bolt of magic my way, narrowly missing me.

I felt Lorandir gathering his magic in preparation. The shield fell as suddenly as it had appeared and the magic user cried out in triumph as his bolt made it through. Lorandir jumped out of the way, spinning agilely to send his own blast of power towards the cultist.

I held Bane tightly and moved towards the other one. He sidestepped my first swing and brought his blade round quickly. I managed to parry his blow and his hood fell down at the impact, revealing greasy long hair and grey skin. Troll. He bared his teeth and stabbed at me wildly. I tried to block the blows, moving gracelessly as I evaded them, clanging Bane's blade against the serrated knife.

Over his shoulder, I saw the magic user laugh nastily and aim a bolt of magic towards the crowd of people, still gathered in the field, although those closest to us were pressing to get away from the fight. I dodged another blow from the troll and ran to get in the path of the magic, activating the shield rune on my own axe as I went.

I made it just in time, the bolt crackling as it connected with the shield. Screams came from behind me as the mass of people felt the power that had almost hit them.

A booming voice rang out over the sounds of our battle, "Solstice is sacred!"

I felt magic sizzle from the direction of the crowd, but Bane's barrier protected me. The cultists and Lorandir were slammed to the ground in a swirl of green magic. They fought to stand up but the power was too strong and they were pinned. I ran over to Lorandir, the force dissipating as soon as he was within the shield my axe provided. I offered him a hand and he gave me a lopsided grin in thanks as he took it and pulled himself up.

I looked across the site, similar vortexes of green magic arced over the henge at two other locations. Schiztz. I guessed that was where the others had placed their speakers and they were in trouble too.

The crowd was screaming now and stampeding to get out of the field. I caught sight of stewards ushering people towards the exit. No one wanted to risk leaving the shelter of the stones in our direction. Ropes appeared from thin air and wrapped themselves around the robed figures. The green force dissipated, vanishing as quickly as it had arrived.

I deactivated the shield and walked over to the magic user. The ropes hummed with power as they dampened his own magic. Whoever had conjured them knew what they were doing. I used Bane's blade to pull back the hood and narrowed my eyes at the wizard who looked back at me. His brown eyes stared at me with glee.

"You fools," he cackled.

I resisted the urge to slap his face, "What are you doing here?"

"Being a distraction!" he laughed again.

I looked at Lorandir, "The speakers!"

While we had been distracted, the speakers had continued to emit their strange frequency across the site and into the ground.

The earth was still vibrating. I sprinted over to it. The elf beat me to it and swung his sword at the electronic device. It sliced it cleanly, but the sound continued to emanate from it, powered by the sorcerer's magic.

I swung Bane hard at the remains of the speaker, bringing my axe down again and again until it was completely destroyed and electrical innards were scattered across the dewy grass. The sound sputtered and then stopped.

I high-fived the elf in celebration. Then his face fell. He knelt on the ground and listened carefully then shook his head at me.

Schiztz. The other speakers. We ran to where the closest arc of green magic had curved to the ground, close to a single stone in front of the standing circle, directly in front of the sunrise. Lorandir raced ahead, his long legs and better fitness levels meant he arrived there well before I reached our friends with Errol in tow. I panted as he filled them in on our fight.

Three other robed figures lay squirming on the ground here too, tied with the same magical ropes that had entrapped our cultists. I saw blood oozing from claw marks through the torn robes.

I couldn't see Agent Jones anywhere but a large cat was sitting next to Dot, its amber eyes narrowed as it considered the elf's words. A shifter. I couldn't pinpoint the animal at first, it had large tufted black ears and thick short fur. Not a type of shifter I'd seen before. A vague memory surfaced from the nature programmes my Mum watched. Lynx. No one else was commenting on the newcomer so I guessed it was one of Agent Jones' contacts.

I turned around as Lorandir spoke and noticed the speaker here was still on, booming its low tones. I passed Errol's lead to Aloora and hefted my axe again.

"No!" I heard Maxi's cry as I smashed the speaker. He knelt on the ground, cradling the broken electronics as I took out some anger on the remaining pieces, making sure it was definitely turned off. It was therapeutic.

The rest of the taskforce stared at me as I finished up, out of breath and using Bane as a prop to recover from the exertion.

"What?" I asked.

The lynx shifted into Agent Jones, "Right, now that Amethyst has got her anger issues out. We need to cut out the other speaker. Maxi, Dot, disconnect it." They raced off. Dot blurred slightly as she used her vampiric speed.

"Did you make anything out while you were listening?" she directed the question at us. I was still having difficulty processing the fact that she was a shifter and I hadn't picked up on it.

"No. But you're a shifter? How…?"

She glared at me and Lorandir took up the conversation. "It might have been words but I didn't understand the language."

"Aloora, you're the language expert. Get rid of that wyrm and get your ear to the ground. Lorandir, tell her any sounds you heard."

I took Errol back from my friend and, as he scrambled back up to my shoulder, I used the opportunity to surreptitiously pull my goggles over my eyes and stare at Agent Jones. Nope, no magical signature that I could sense or see. I glanced towards the fleeing crowds. Their auras lit up the fields through my tinted goggles. They were still working then. I noticed two figures walking in our direction with intense auras.

I gripped Bane and lifted my goggles and was surprised to see Madam Mim and an elderly man with a close cut beard and dressed in a druidic robe walking towards us. He carried a twisted staff in one hand, not like a walking stick I noticed, more like a weapon.

"It is worse than we feared," Madam Mim spoke grimly without preamble as she reached Agent Jones and me. "I can feel the energies shifting, we don't have long."

"Can you contain it?" Agent Jones asked bluntly.

"I don't know, but we will do our best."

Agent Jones nodded in reply and the two figures stood either side of the smaller standing stone directly aligned with the sunrise and raised their arms, gathering magic to them.

"What's going on? Who's he? What are they going to do? How are you a shifter? What is happening?" The questions tumbled out of me.

Agent Jones gave me an appraising look, as if weighing up how much to tell me then she sighed and rubbed the back of her neck, "It looks like someone's trying to waken the dragon we think is underneath Stonehenge. Merlin and Mim are going to try to use their magic to put the dragon back to sleep. I'm a shifter in the normal way, but you can't sense me because of this." She held up her arm, pointing to her wrist where the gold band with a cat's head lay.

I looked closer and noted that the cat was shaped like a lynx. A magical dampener. I was alight with a crafter's curiosity but had the sense to restrain myself from asking further questions. She was clearly sensitive about shifting or she wouldn't be wearing such an item.

Instead I shifted back a couple of responses, “Merlin and Morgan?”

Agent Jones nodded. I stared at the magic users, who now had green and blue light streaming from their hands as they cast their spells. Their hair and clothing whirled around them like they were in a vortex of power. The stone circle was now empty of all bar the last stragglers, who were clamouring to get out of the area.

I looked back at Aloora and Lorandir lying on the ground. He was mouthing words to her and she had her eyes closed, concentrating.

A magical field settled over the stone circle. It was suddenly strangely silent after the racket of the Solstice celebrations. Even the birds were quiet, their dawn chorus stopped out of respect for, or fear of, the magic expended.

Chapter 15

As the silence continued, I released the breath I hadn't realised I was holding. I tore my gaze from the standing stones and the two sorcerers illuminated by the pinkish orange dawn light.

I smiled as I turned, blinking at the bright sun that was now nearly fully over the horizon, but it turned into a grimace as I saw Aloora and Lorandir still pressed to the ground. Errol dug his claws painfully into my shoulder and emitted a low growl.

Aloora got up finally and walked over to Agent Jones. She shrugged apologetically. "I think there are words there but no one has heard Draconic spoken by dragons themselves in millennia. I'm relying on Lorandir's interpretations of the sounds and Draconic is a contextual language…I'd only be guessing."

"Well what's your best guess?" Agent Jones pinched the bridge of her nose in frustration.

"My best guess is that it's not good. The rumbling is getting stronger and I think if there's something down there, it's awake and confused."

Errol was bobbing up and down now, alternately whining in my ear and blowing small flickers of flame at the henge. "Er, I think Errol agrees with your guess. He's pretty agitated."

Agent Jones narrowed her eyes at my pet wyrm and stepped closer. He sniffed her hand as she held it out to him, but then continued to look over her shoulder to where Mim and Merlin were standing.

Dot materialised at Agent Jones' side in a blur of speed. "Speaker destroyed."

Agent Jones nodded. At that point, Errol let out an anguished roar right next to my ear. I swore loudly. As I was about to tell him off, the ground shook, more violently than before. I was having trouble keeping my footing.

Mim and Merlin swayed slightly, still pouring magic into the stone circle. The shaking stopped for a moment. Then the ground reverberated forcefully. The two magic users staggered backwards as they were forced out of the circle.

I ran over to help them get clear of the stones, Agent Jones close behind me.

"We can't hold it," Mim breathed. Schiztz. I hurried her forward, to the edge of the grassy field and the safety of a large stone.

The stones began to tremble, the magic field dissipating as the force from beneath the ground increased. The monoliths then quaked as the ground imploded. The earth crumbled down and a gaping hole appeared.

There was a sighing sound as if the planet itself was holding its breath and then, slowly, swaying slightly and blinking in the dawn light, a huge crested head appeared. I was expecting the same creature I had seen emerge from under Cardiff Castle, but this dragon was much bigger. Its pale white scales reflected the light, making it seem like it was the embodiment of the Solstice sun.

It opened its huge jaws, threw its head back and roared to the sky. I cringed at the primal sound and involuntarily took a step backwards. Its clawed front feet gripped the edge of the hole and it slithered upwards out of the ground. Once out in the open, its true scale was enormous. I craned my neck upwards to try to take it all in. Its long tail still trailed into the dark cavern. It was truly, terrifyingly awesome.

It beat its wings several times, reminding me of Errol trying to stretch himself after a long sleep.

"The white dragon has risen," Merlin spoke in a strained voice. I felt the change in energy as Merlin gathered power to him and a blast of magical lightning shot from his hands towards the creature. The dragon roared again as the bolt of magic connected with its chest.

It flapped its large wings and took flight, gusts of wind hitting us with each down stroke. The temperature cooled. Suddenly, instead of the growing heat of a summer's day, it felt like a crisp winter's morning. I shivered despite my jacket and warm blood.

As it hovered above us, its jewelled green eyes alit on Merlin with hatred and it opened its mouth and breathed ice directly at him. I was close enough to the sorcerer to see the exhaustion lines in his face as he raised his arms to defend himself. I activated the shield rune on my axe, praying that it would work and stepped in front of the old man.

The icy cold hit me hard, buffeting the invisible shield in front of me. The icy onslaught continued and I felt the barrier's energy falter. "Move!" I shouted to the magician and he staggered away. The ice entombed me. It was most like plunging into cold water when you're not expecting it. I fought to control my thoughts through the panic setting in as I found I couldn't move. I couldn't breathe either. Schiztz.

As I struggled against the icy tomb, I felt heat emanating from Errol. He was desperately breathing fire, trying to melt the dragon's ice that encased us. That little wyrm brought me some hope and a little room to draw a breath as the ice closest to my face and shoulder melted.

I heard something metallic scrape along the outside of the thick ice walls. Someone was trying to get us out. Hope swelled through me again. Briefly. It flickered out when I realised I couldn't even see through the ice, it was that thick. It would take too long to melt or cut their way in.

Finally, I remembered my axe, frozen in my hands. I spoke the word to activate the fire rune carved into its metallic head and felt it heat under my palms. I focused on that heat now coursing along the blade and muttered the Dwarfish word for fire again and again, feeling the ice around me turn to water. Soon, I was able to move and I pushed the axe against the wall I had heard the scraping through and moved slowly forward. Errol jumped down to be closer to the heated weapon and added his flames.

It felt like an age but we finally met Dot on the other side, doing something similar but less effective with the enchanted sword she held.

"Thank goodness!" She hugged me spontaneously as I crawled my way through the gap we had made and inelegantly landed in a puddle on the floor. I looked up and shivered at the large spiky ice crystals protruding from the ground. That could have been my tomb.

The dragon was blasting its icy breath at two shapes as they darted about underneath it. I recognised a large cat form and the slim elven figure distracting it. Mim and Merlin were loosing bolts of magic from behind the larger stones, now leaning precariously but providing some form of protection. I looked around for Aloora and found my best friend crouching by a stone with Maxi holding a smartphone and a sword. Unbelievably she was filming the whole thing, a look of academic interest on her face. I swore under my breath and did a strange crablike ducking run over to where they were hiding. Dot slowed her pace to match mine so we arrived at the hiding place together.

I was annoyed that Aloora was on her phone at a time like this, "I know this is great social media content, but you two are the dragon and communications experts, is there anything that can help us?"

Aloora gave me a hurt look. "Agent Jones asked me to film this and guard him. I tried yelling at it to 'Stop' in Draconic but it was pretty pissed after Merlin shot lightning at it."

"Sorry, I shouldn't have assumed," I patted her shoulder.

She shrugged, "In your defence, you were just frozen!"

Maxi was hugging his legs to his body muttering, "It wasn't supposed to happen," over and over again with a wild look in his eyes.

"What's up with him?" I asked, keeping my eye on the game of chase playing out in front of us.

"Apparently, he fiddled with some settings on those speakers and the comms devices on the orders of the Office's superiors. It's basically his fault this is happening, isn't that right Maxi?" Dot jabbed him painfully in the shoulder, then turned her attention back to the battle raging in front of us.

I looked at him, surprised, he hadn't seemed like the type to be part of a crazy cult or betray the team. Madam Mim's words from the fortune telling came back to me, "*Betrayal*," she had hissed at him, "*but who is the betrayer and who is the betrayed?*" I shivered and this time it was nothing to do with the cold.

Dot caught my eye, "I'm going in." She blurred with speed as she raced towards the dragon. She launched herself off one of the stones and activated the fire rune on her enchanted sword again. She managed to graze the dragon's tail. It screeched that ear-splitting roar and rushed upwards, beating its wings strongly to get away.

I left Errol with Aloora, trusting that he'd be happier further away from the dragons and I moved closer, running. As if I could add anything to a vampire, a shifter and an elf, I chided myself internally. I kept going though. I wasn't about to let them get killed if I could help. I reached them just as the dragon dove down, sending an icy blast towards Dot. She jumped and rolled, avoiding the main impact but I saw one of the crystals pierce her leg.

The ground began to rumble again, shaking dangerously. "What the dzrak?" I spoke aloud. The vibrations grew. There seemed to be a rhythm to them, a pounding, thumping noise that shook the ground every second or so. Footsteps. Schiztz.

Another dragon's head, smaller this time, peeped from the cavernous hole in the ground. It gave a small barking noise followed by a chirp. The larger dragon swooped down and perched on the edge of the hole, causing the ground to jolt with force.

The shock of its landing reverberated through the stone circle. I watched as, in slow motion, one of the larger upright stones still standing started to tilt precariously. Lorandir was in its path with his back to the danger. Without thinking, I yelled "No!" and launched myself towards the stone, placing myself between it and the elf.

He turned dumbly to stare at me. "Move!" I shouted. I faced the stone. It was just above me, no time to move. I closed my eyes and impotently raised my axe over my head as if I could stop it crushing me.

I felt power course through me, the amethyst in my back pocket heating. The stone stopped its fall an inch above my outstretched hands with a metallic scrape as it touched Bane's blade. It seemed to glow, a strange purple light pulsing over it as it hovered there. Experimentally, I reached out and touched the monolith. It felt warm and smooth from centuries of people touching it and it stayed where it was, leaning at an impossible angle above me.

I had the crazy notion that I could control the stone and tentatively moved my hands. It responded, grinding against the ground as it shifted position. I felt my hair stand on end with power I had never experienced before and willed it to go back to a standing position.

Slowly, weightily, it obeyed and reversed its fall. As it settled into its new upright position, I walked up to it and patted it gently as if it had done a good job. I could almost imagine a sense of pride emanating from the large boulder. I turned and was conscious of everyone staring at me.

I looked around and nonchalantly stepped away from the stone, as if it was perfectly natural to control monoliths that weighed several tonnes.

The dragons were also looking at me with narrowed eyes. I bit my lip. We were at some sort of impasse I didn't understand and I didn't want to make the wrong move. I lifted my hand in a gesture of peace.

That was the wrong thing to do. The larger dragon took flight again with a shriek and the smaller one followed it. They dived in tandem and delivered short icy blasts across the field, turning their heads from left to right as they peppered the ground with ice crystals.

I dived to avoid the attack and ran to shelter behind the rock I had just controlled. I leant against it, suddenly feeling weak, my breath coming in short pants as if I had just sprinted a marathon. I felt a searing pain in my arm, an ice crystal had exploded upwards from the ground at a strange angle and had pierced my skin. I cried out as my mouth caught up with the pain and wrenched myself free, tearing my muscle even more.

After the second pass over the henge, the large dragon stopped its attack suddenly, hovering above us. The smaller one did a loop around it and beat its wings to stay close to its side. Both creatures turned their heads in a westerly direction, ignoring us all. I peeked out from behind the monolith, cradling my useless arm and cocked my head involuntarily as I strained to hear what had distracted them.

The large dragon made a strange sound, a cross between a growl and a rumble. If I didn't know better, I'd have called it a croon, a sort of wistful sound. Then it beat its wings strongly and flew west, away from the morning sun. The smaller dragon flying in its wake. We watched the creatures as they climbed, quickly gaining altitude. They flew out of sight rapidly, glinting gold as their pale scales reflected the light.

The summer's heat hit me as quickly as it had left, promising to be another scorching hot day.

Lorandir walked over to thank me for saving him. I headed him off with a "Don't even worry about it." He gave me a strange look and reached out to touch my injured arm with his cool hand. I felt the intoxicating, heady sense of his magic covering me. The familiar pleasant rush of honey mead, bittersweet chocolate and fresh forests washing over me as he healed me. I could feel the torn muscle knitting itself back together under his touch.

The greenish golden glow of his magic expanded beyond my arm and throughout my whole body. I could feel my own energy returning and I felt good. As if I'd had a full night's sleep and hadn't lifted a standing stone weighing twenty five tonnes. "Thank you," I murmured, absently leaning into him. I was feeling a little light-headed and drunk from the power he had poured into me.

"Don't even worry about it," he replied coolly with a lopsided half smile. In the early daylight, his blonde hair seemed to glow as if he were some sort of angel. I felt myself grinning back. The moment lengthened, then I remembered the others and broke our connection, feeling self-conscious again. I turned to Agent Jones, looking for direction.

She had shifted back to her human form and was gazing upwards in the direction the dragons had flown. As I watched, she swept an appraising eye over the chaos left of Stonehenge and the cringing captives tied up. She pinched the bridge of her nose and let out a long-suffering sigh. I had a feeling that was the closest she got to losing it in the field.

"Right. Let's wrap this up." She strode over to where Aloora was putting her smartphone away and trying to look menacing as Maxi's guard. Agent Jones narrowed her eyes, and I thought her pupils narrowed into slits as she glared at him, "I'll deal with you later." She dismissed Maxi and pulled out her phone and made a call.

Within fifteen minutes, a van had pulled up directly at the gates of Stonehenge and several muscled Magical Liaison Officers were sprinting into the field. I could sense their magical gear as they grabbed the cultists and roughly marched them to the van.

Chapter 16

We caught the news on the van's radio on the drive back. Dot was sitting next to Maxi in the back, hand on her sword and looking grim. Maxi himself looked awful. His mad professor style hair was even more dishevelled and he gazed despondently out of the window at the fields rolling past.

Madam Mim was upfront, next to Agent Jones who was driving in silence. For once, a slight frown played over the sorcerer's brow.

Aloora was eagerly showing me the footage on her phone. It was strange, watching a film of the events. It had all seemed to take a lot longer that the few minutes her recording showed. I cringed as I saw myself jump in front of the monolith and my hair stand on end as power coursed through me. The footage didn't pick up magic per se but at one point I turned to face the camera and my eyes were glowing purple.

"Do not post that on your social media channel!" Errol grunted as my hands stopped stroking the small wyrm. He was as glad as I was to be alive and was showing it by being extra affectionate to the point where I was very glad I had a fire charm as he kept blowing small, happy bursts of fire as he sat in my lap.

Aloora rolled her eyes at me, "Of course not. But what happened? I didn't know you could do that."

I shifted uncomfortably in my seat and lowered my voice, even though practically everyone on the taskforce had superhuman hearing, "I have no idea. I moved a dzraking standing stone with my mind Ally!"

She tapped her hand to her cheek thoughtfully, "I haven't read much about dwarven magic in my studies…it looked like you had a direct link to the stone somehow." I shrugged. My friend was already lost in thought about a new possible route of academic study. I just didn't want to be a case study or a pet project.

My head nodded forward as the van rolled along the smooth road back towards Madam Mim's cottage. Merlin had stayed at Stonehenge to supervise the proper repositioning of the stones with a group of helpful wizards who had materialised after the danger had passed. There was a story there I didn't understand. I felt myself being lulled to sleep.

Aloora prodded me awake as the van pulled up outside the house. People were scurrying around, fleeing away from the site of the standing stones at Avebury. Agent Jones leapt out of the car and grabbed a woman dressed in a flowing skirt.

“What’s going on?” she demanded as the rest of us piled out of the vehicle.

“The ground, it was shaking…the stones…” Agent Jones let go of the terrified woman and sprinted towards the stone circle. I forced my body into a run and followed her. Lorandir sprinted past me and easily kept pace with the shifter. I stopped as we arrived at the circle, leaning on my knees as I caught my breath. Today was easily the most cardio I had done in a year.

The field was empty of people and several stones had fallen over. I surveyed the scene and noticed a small mound of fresh earth pushing up through the grass. Errol gave it a sniff and sat down. I climbed it.

“Hey, this is weir…” I fell through the ground and landed hard in a deep, underground cavern. “…” I was too winded to swear.

“Are you alright down there?”

I looked up at the chink of light from the hole I had fallen through. “Just peachy!” I wheezed. I forced myself to sit up, wincing at the sharp pain in my ribs. I gingerly tested my legs and found I could stand.

“We’re getting a rope,” Agent Jones’ head disappeared from the hole.

I didn’t bother to reply and instead looked around. The shaft of light illuminated the cavern. It was a large space, with a domed roof. I hobbled around. It looked like it had been dug out using tools. I followed the wall until it opened into a tunnel. I found a large white scale on the floor at the tunnel entrance and picked it up. It glittered in the little morning light that shone into the cave.

“What’s down there?” Aloora’s voice cracked through the communicator I had forgotten I was wearing.

“Er, not much. It’s a cave, not a natural one. I guess this is where the small dragon was sleeping. I found a scale.”

“Lucky!” Typical response from my dragon mad friend. I rolled my eyes at the device.

A rope dropped through the ceiling and coiled onto the floor. I walked slowly towards it, grimacing with each step and holding my side.

I looked at the rope. There was no way I could climb up, even if I wasn’t injured. I stared up at the opening.

“I can’t climb that!”

I heard Agent Jones’ sigh. She pulled up the rope and a few minutes later it reappeared with a harness attached. “Pull twice when you’re ready and we’ll pull you up.” I stepped into the harness, trying to ignore the pain as I tightened it.

I gave two sharp pulls on the rope and was immediately hoisted upwards. I swung wildly with no control and focused on gripping onto the rope. At the top, strong hands pulled me the last way and I grunted in pain as I bumped onto the ground.

That familiar healing magic swept over me again and I inhaled deeply. “You’re a handy elf to have around,” I murmured without thinking. I was rewarded by that grin again before Aloora swept me into a huge hug.

“Stop getting into dangerous situations!” she admonished me.

I shrugged, “It’s not like I ask for it!”

Errol licked my face with his rough tongue and nuzzled his head against me as I stroked his neck. “Don’t worry boy, I’m still here.”

Agent Jones had pulled some warning cones and tape from somewhere, despite only carrying her crocodile skin handbag, and was setting them up round the hole. She waved us away as she made another call.

Errol wound his way between my legs as we walked back to the cottage, pleased to have me back. The second time I stumbled, I picked up the wyrm and carried him the rest of the way.

I flopped down into a comfy chair as soon as we got in. Madam Mim bustled in with a tray of teas. She handed me a large mug of strong English tea. It smelled sweeter than I usually like my tea, but I took a sip and instantly felt better.

We sipped our tea in silence, a mood of despondency settling over us. We were alive and, thanks to elven healing magic, unharmed, but there were now another two dragons loose in Britain.

Agent Jones stamped in and scanned the room. "You. Upstairs. I want answers." She barked at Maxi and then stormed upstairs. He trudged after her, looking at the floor as if he couldn't meet our eyes. I felt a pang of sympathy for him.

When the shouting started, I forced myself outside. I didn't want to listen. The others followed. It turned out that Agent Jones could shout really loud so we walked behind the trailing roses into the strange forested part of the garden.

Errol ran off among the trees, sniffing and scrabbling happily. "Come back!" I called after him.

"Do not worry, no harm can come to him here," Madam Mim spoke softly yet assuredly. I saw Errol pounce at a golden red bird that was perched on a low hanging branch. Mid-leap, the bird transformed into flames. The wyrm tried to turn in the air and ended up hitting the tree hard. The bird hopped down to him and chirruped in a way that sounded like laughter. "Well, no harm that isn't of his own making anyway."

"Wha…" I started.

"A phoenix!" Aloora squealed as she moved closer. Errol was now blowing his own flicker of flames towards the bird and it was preening itself as it enjoyed the fire. "They're extinct!"

"Not here," There was something in the way she said 'here' that made me think Madam Mim wasn't talking about Wiltshire.

"Where is here exactly?" I asked.

"It is my home. I am always connected to this realm, a place for weary travellers of true heart to rest and heal. A sanctuary for those who are deserving. It has many names, this Land of Apples, but Avalon is one you may have heard of."

Aloora's head snapped back from the phoenix to Madam Mim. "The same Avalon where Arthur is supposed to be?"

Madam Mim nodded serenely. "Where Arthur is," she corrected.

Suddenly something clicked in my brain. "Excalibur!" I burst out. The famed sword was legendary of course, and was the subject of many dwarfish texts. Forged by an unknown weapons master, the sword was created here in Avalon before being presented to the fabled king.

It was said to be so brilliant that it blinded all enemies when it was drawn and blazed fire from chimeras etched into its hilt. Its beautiful scabbard was more powerful still as the wearer could not bleed from wounds dealt whilst wearing the scabbard.

I had doodled that blade for hours on my notebook as a teenager, trying to work out the complex charms or enchantments that would enable it to do all that the legends told. To find out that it was so close was tantalising.

"Of course a talented metalsmith would know all about that sword," Madam Mim shook her head, "It ultimately caused so many problems, I swore never again to allow it in the mortal world. Far better it is kept here with Arthur, the only man who could wield it righteously."

My head was reeling. "So it's here? Can we see it?"

Madam Mim looked thoughtful, "Not at this time."

Aloora looked as if she'd just solved a complicated translation. She opened her mouth to say something when Agent Jones burst in on us. "We're leaving after lunch," she stated before turning and stalking back the way she'd come.

Madam Mim sighed then led the way back inside for food. She didn't disappoint, seemingly conjuring delicious quiches, sandwiches and scotch eggs from empty cupboards. I dug in and grabbed a large wedge of fruit cake for desert. It was full of plump sultanas and juicy cherries and I savoured every bite, wondering if I could cram a piece somewhere into my backpack to take home.

I decided it would be too messy, even wrapped in a napkin and looked longingly at the remaining slices before heading upstairs to pack. Aloora joined me while Errol sunbathed on the windowsill.

"How weird is it that Madam Mim has access to Avalon?" I was folding my clothes haphazardly and stuffing them into my backpack but still caught my friend's eye roll.

"It's not weird at all. She rules the place."

"Madam Mim?! Purveyor of potions?" I was pleased with that alliteration.

"She might be calling herself Madam Mim but the only enchantress who lives in Avalon is Morgan."

I stared at Aloora. Sometimes I was exceedingly slow and she was too clever for me to keep up.

"Morgan le Fay. Arthur's sister, or half-sister, I suppose," she mused, "ruler of Avalon." I still looked confused and she gave an exasperated snort. "I thought you liked Arthurian legends."

"I like Excalibur," I responded peevishly, "hang on, so do you think that Merlin was, y'know, the real Merlin?!"

"Could very well be."

"Dzrak me! We just met *the* Merlin!" I was speechless then I groaned, "I wish I'd said something cool to him."

Aloora giggled. I went into the bathroom, still shaking my head in disbelief as I grabbed my hairbrush from the side of the sink.

"Wotcha beautiful! What's goin' on then?"

I groaned, I had forgotten about Gary. "Er, we're just packing up, heading home, so…you'll have the bathroom back to yourself now."

"That's a shame. I enjoyed sharing it with two lovely ladies," he gave a lewd wink. It was almost impressive that he made it look dirty given that he was part of the bath, "until next time then love."

This was a really weird cottage. I grabbed my things, shoved Bane into the empty carry all that had previously contained the stock I had made for Agent Jones and walked downstairs. I was the first one down and decided to have a final look in the garden. Dumping my things on a sofa, I walked outside and meandered down the path.

I stopped at each potted herb and pinched a little piece between my fingers before bringing it up to my nose. I recognised fragrant lavender and the thyme reminded me of roast chicken dinners. I was twiddling a leaf between my fingers trying to recall the name of the plant with such a familiar scent as I neared the trailing roses.

I was suddenly aware of a voice on the other side. Agent Jones. She sounded very annoyed.

"I am not coming back into the office if what Maxi told me was true." She practically shouted at whoever was on the phone. I backed away as quietly as I could and headed inside.

Chapter 17

The couple of hours in the van on the way back were uneventful. The news was already reporting a bomb scare in Stonehenge and a gas leak in Avebury and warning people to stay away from both as roadblocks were in place. The Magical Liaison Office are very efficient at getting their press releases out.

Agent Jones pressed a button and nineties pop replaced the newsreader's voice. I was a little surprised that she would have this type of station pre-programmed into the radio and idly wondered if she had ever been clubbing. I couldn't picture her bopping away in a club wearing one of her fitted suits, although maybe she owned other clothes…somehow I couldn't see it.

She thoughtfully dropped Aloora off outside her Victorian house on Miskin Street and I gave a cheery wave as she let herself in.

Next stop was the main road outside Cardiff Castle, which still had a 'closed for renovation' sign hung on its wooden gate. I had heard that they had managed to get a grant towards rebuilding the destroyed part of the castle when the dragon had awakened here earlier in the year.

Agent Jones pulled up sharply on a kerb in a no waiting zone and I manhandled my bag out of the van, swearing as Errol pulled on his lead, anxious to get home. Lorandir got out too and easily shouldered his own backpack.

I waved as the van pulled into traffic and was gone without a word, taking Dot and Maxi to the Magical Liaison Office headquarters in Cardiff.

"Well…see you then," I set off towards my shop. He fell into step beside me. "Er…where are you heading?"

He gave me a small smile, "I thought I'd say hi to Marco while I'm in town. He's working at your shop, right?"

I nodded and kept walking. I didn't know they were still in touch. The silence felt awkward. After biting my lip, trying to think of something to say, I tried: "So…Aloora thinks Madam Mim is really Morgan le Fay…"

He considered this, "Could be."

I gave up after that and kept quiet for the remaining short distance to my shop cum flat.

"So, 'ow was the girls' road trip?" Marco asked cheerfully as I opened the door to a familiar tinkling sound. He'd replaced the bell. I waved, noting the pot plant he'd rescued from my flat now flourishing on the counter. I hoped he was taking it back with him. The only plants I managed to keep alive were Mucklewhite mushrooms, which seemed to enjoy neglect in my small kitchen.

Those weren't the only changes he'd made. I froze partway into the shop and stared in shock at the mural on the wall. Lorandir walked into me as I stood blocking the entrance. I weakly moved forward, further into the shop. Errol tugged his lead free from my unprotesting hand and scurried to the forge where I heard him chomping on coal happily.

I blinked. The painting was still there.

"…" I had no words.

"You like it, yes?"

"…"

I stared at it then at Marco. He was nodding happily at my reaction. I turned to Lorandir. The bloody elf was smirking.

"It's very…Dwarfish," the elf commented neutrally. Traitor.

"Marco…I…how?"

He waved his hand dismissively as he walked over and embraced us each in turn, "It was no trouble. The shop 'as been very quiet so I had plenty of time, and the muse, she came to me."

"I think I need to sit down," I replied, weakly. I moved to the swivel chair behind the shabby chic counter. Maybe it wouldn't look so bad from this angle. Nope. It was still there, still massive and still unsightly.

Marco had painted an entire wall of my minimalist, chic shop with a giant fantasy mural of epic proportions. It showed a buxom dwarfish lady, complete with helmet, ornamental sword and leather armour. She was giving a saucy wink and next to her, in graffiti style lettering, were the words 'welcome to Amethyst's Treasures' in neon purple paint. I squinted. The dwarf looked a little like me, although with better hair, all done up into complicated braids. Lorandir was looking at it thoughtfully with his head tilted to one side.

"Schiztz Marco, what have you done?"

"I know, she is impressive, no? I showed the sketch to your Dad. 'E loved it."

Dad had been in on this and hadn't called? I decided to move closer, maybe it would be better if I could take it in slowly, focus on the small details. The picture was wearing my fire charm earrings and a silver bracelet I recognised from one of my current collections. At least it was vaguely related to jewellery. I hadn't realised Marco was so good at painting. If I looked at it objectively, it was nicely done and if I saw it on a book, I'd think it was a cool cover. I blinked again.

"Marco…does she have a beard?" I had originally thought the plaits with silver bands were all hair, but they merged under her chin.

He nodded eagerly.

I was saved from replying by a couple of students pushing open the door. They ignored the glass cases and stared at the picture. "Cool."

"Get a selfie, I've got to put this on Insta," his mate replied, taking out a smartphone. They posed in front of the mural with big thumbs up.

"Who's the artist?" the first student asked. I pointed weakly and Marco stepped forward. In another surge of excitement, they took selfies with him too and promised to follow him online. I leant against the staircase to my flat. This was a lot to take in when all I really wanted was a shower without a pervy gargoyle in the bathroom and a sugary snack. I thought longingly of Brinda's brownies at the Dragon's Head or red velvet cupcakes from the café in Royal Arcade.

"Hey, cool, how much is this?"

I turned to see what they were looking at. One of the more ornamental swords I hadn't taken with me to Avebury had been mounted on the wall. I stared at it; my weapons business was meant to be under the counter not on display for students to purchase.

Marco jumped in as I was clearly unable to form a coherent sentence and gave a ridiculously high price. The student took it from the display and began swinging it around, imagining he was fighting an invisible enemy. By the way he handled the blade, my money was on the imaginary enemy. That was enough for me.

"No sword fighting in the shop! If you break it, you buy it!" I squealed.

The student looked sheepish and put the sword carefully on the counter, his touch lingering on the engraved hilt. "Sorry, I'll take it."

"…" I was back to being speechless. The amount Marco had charged was ridiculous and he wasn't even haggling.

Marco rang up the purchase with a smile, "Your sword is too big for the bags."

I blinked at him, unsure whether that was an innuendo, but it was true too, the small paper bags in the shop were designed for jewellery not weapons. I shook Bane free of the carry all and offered that up.

"You can't walk across town with a naked blade without a weapon's permit..."

His friend looked at my axe, now leaning against the bannister and made to touch it, "How much for that one?"

“Not for sale!” I jumped back in front of my ancestral axe protectively. The student looked shocked and Marco glared at me. I plastered back on my shopkeeper’s smile and moved Bane behind the counter.

Now I was next to Marco, I bumped him deliberately to relieve some of my frustration. I ran my hand down either side of the sword’s blade as I put it into the army surplus carry all, using my magic to blunt the edge so the most the budding sword fighter could do was bruise someone. I didn’t want any student blood on my hands. It was lucky this sword had been too flashy for my other clientele’s tastes and I hadn’t put any enchantments on it.

I handed the bag over to the satisfied customer, nearly knocking over the leafy plant on the counter. Marco grabbed it and placed it carefully in another, less prominent spot. The student left grinning and talking to his friend about how badass the sword was.

“Tag it on social media!” Marco called after them.

“I don’t even have social media for the shop!” I hissed, grabbing on to the tiny bit of normality I had left here.

Marco shrugged, “I set it up for you, see.” He passed me his phone and there was indeed an account for my shop. It was covered with pictures of the mural in progress. I was slightly surprised to see some tastefully posed photos of actual stock as well. At least that was more on brand. He clicked something and a hashtag popped up with a number of photos showing people posing in front of the finished picture and leaving the shop with purchases.

“People love the mural. They come in to see it, they buy, they leave,” he made it sound so simple.

"Thank you for looking after my shop," I said belatedly, giving him a hug. I was rewarded with a broad smile. "You'll have to teach me how to use that app."

"Of course, now I have an 'ot date. Ciao." Marco picked up a designer scarf from the back of the swivel chair and wrapped it round his neck before blowing me and Lorandir an air kiss and sweeping out of the door. I sank down into the chair weakly.

"Well it does bring in customers," the elf smiled at me.

I gave him a look in return. I didn't know if the worst part was that I couldn't get rid of it without offending my friend or that he was right.

I ran through a number of responses in my head and finally settled for, "I need a drink."

His grin grew at that, "Shall we head to the pub?"

The elven cul took a surreptitious picture on his phone on the way out. I huffed and hurried on before he asked me to pose in front of it.

I led the way to the Rummer, wanting familiar territory and possibly a large piece of their chocolate fudge cake to go with my drink. Lorandir bought the first round and I took a large swig, still dazed from what Marco had done to my shop in less than a week.

"It doesn't look as bad as you think it does, you know," he offered.

I sighed, "It's just not me,"

"I think it is you," he pointed out unhelpfully.

I glared at him, causing him to laugh, "I don't have a beard! And you know what I mean, it's not my style. It's not what I thought my shop would be."

He leant in close to inspect my chin, and touched my cheek gently, I could feel my face start to redden and pulled away. "No beard," he agreed, "what did you want your shop to be?"

He was surprisingly easy to talk to, especially after I'd practically downed my first drink and bought us another round, along with two slices of cake. I found myself outlining all my aspirations. How I wanted to start my own shop to make Dad proud, how I'd dreamed it would be sleek and sophisticated, how I wanted to invent something unique – like unloseable jewellery. I even told the elf that it had been his pendant that had inspired that notion. He seemed pleased about that but shrugged when I pressed him for details about how it was made.

"I don't know really. An elven smith made the pair for me and…" he faltered, unable to say the name of his former friend. I reached out and squeezed his hand for moral support, "…for us, we just had to be there as he made the final adjustments to pour our magic into the metal as he worked it."

I hadn't heard of that technique before and wanted to ask more, but at that point a young waiter turned up with the cakes and plonked them onto the wooden table top. The fudgy sauce was oozing all over the chocolate cake and the generous scoops of vanilla ice cream were slowly sinking into the sauce as they melted. I helped myself to a generous spoonful and let my eyes close as I savoured the taste. I may have moaned slightly.

"Good cake?"

I opened my eyes, slightly annoyed that my cake moment had been interrupted. "Try yours," I pointed my spoon at the untouched bowl in front of Lorandir. He obliged me with a snort of derision which quickly changed into a moan of satisfaction as he tasted the dessert.

"Right?"

"This is possibly the best cake ever," he agreed, scooping up a second spoonful.

"I'll have to introduce you to Brinda's brownies," I said without thinking.

"It's a date," he replied. I murmured something non-committal. A date sounded formal. He noticed my silence and raised his glass, "To more amazing puddings!"

I smiled with relief that he had broken the awkward silence creeping in between us and chinked my glass against his. The vodka and coke tasted too bitter with the sweet cake and I pulled a face before taking another large bite to get rid of the harsh taste.

The dessert was finished too soon and, after scraping the bowl clean with my spoon, I briefly considered ordering another. I decided to restrain myself, but it was a close call.

Lorandir had leant back in the wooden chair, stretching out as he relaxed. "Shall we get some proper food?"

He went up in my estimation and I tried not to sound too keen, "They do a decent steak and chips here."

"And if we stay here, we can always get another portion of cake," he added, going up even further in my estimation. He was turning into a very good friend.

Epilogue

After a companionable meal filled with good conversation and a few more drinks, I was decidedly tipsy. Lorandir walked me home, a perfect gentleman, I thought…until he came in to grab the bag he'd left by the stairs in my shop. Of course, that was why he had come back with me. I walked him back out of the Royal Arcade, the gates were locked to the public after trading hours, so I had to let him out.

There was an awkward moment when we said goodbye at the iron gate. I went for a traditional Dwarfish gesture of clasping wrists and he leaned in for a hug, which meant my hand was pressed against his trousers, uncomfortably close to his groin for a second. After that, I gave an awkward wave as he left.

Once back inside the safety of my shop and alone, away from further chance of embarrassing myself, I gazed at the huge mural again and shuddered. The picture was enormous and even drinking a couple more vodka and cokes than I should have didn't improve it.

Errol gave me a lick of welcome and headed upstairs to go back to sleep. I followed, dragging my backpack with me. After a quick hot shower, I went straight to bed and was soon snoring loudly.

I awoke with a start. Something tugging in my mind. One of my traps had been set off. I heard a strange scuffling sound. Belatedly, I remembered I'd left Bane downstairs behind the counter and had gone to sleep in the nude as I hadn't been bothered to dig out a clean t-shirt to sleep in. Schiztz.

Buoyed by the remaining alcohol in my system I decided enough was enough. I closed my eyes to see if I could sense which trap had been triggered. To my surprise it was one in my bedside table. Someone was right next to me, going through my drawers and I hadn't heard them come in.

I slitted open one eye and thought I could see a shape in my room. I started to roll away as if I was still asleep. Then fear crashed over me in a wave as my brain finally caught on: there was an intruder in my room. Next to my bed. I did a strange crabwalk across the bed, backing away from the figure. I fell onto the hard floor, tangled in my sheets. Grabbing one against me to cover myself, I sprinted over to the light switch.

An elf blinked at me, eyes narrowed against the sudden light. I had partially blinded myself too and it took me several moments to focus.

"Well, are you going to release me?" the female elf asked over her shoulder with a note of irritation. I blinked some more, my foggy brain trying to place where I'd seen her before.

"Why are you in my bedroom?"

The elf shrugged, her long blonde hair swaying with her shoulders. Satisfied she was stuck, I walked downstairs to get my axe. My head was racing. I thought about calling someone but my phone was on my bedside table. Schiztz. I grabbed Bane and padded back upstairs, still gripping the bedsheet around myself like some sort of toga. I held Bane in what I hoped was a threatening manner, at odds with the plain white sheet I was struggling to keep around me.

The elf stared at me. I did a practice swing of my axe, "Why are you in my bedroom?"

"You're holding that wrong you know," the elf was far too calm. "I don't want to hurt you. I was just looking for something."

This was not going how I had planned. I rolled my shoulders back, feeling the beginnings of a stress headache. "Why are you looking for something in my bedroom?"

"I thought he might have given it to you," the elf's confidence seemed to shrink and her voice was soft. Suddenly I recognised her. Espretha. Lorandir's friend. The one who had abandoned him to join a cult. I still had no idea why she was here. "Please, release me and I'll be gone, I mean you no harm," she held out her free hand to show me she didn't have any weapons in it. Her other hand was stuck in my underwear drawer.

"Given me what?" I drew my eyebrows together in confusion.

Espretha sank onto my bed and shining tears began to run down her face. Schiztz. I was not good at dealing with emotional outbursts. I resorted to the only thing I could think of, "Would you like a cup of tea?"

She nodded miserably. I grabbed the first bit of clothing I could find - an oversized dirty hoody with a superhero printed on it and a plain pair of pants - and went to put the kettle on, “How do you take it?”

“Black with sugar please,” she replied shakily.

I got dressed in the kitchen and made the drinks, giving her a plain mug. I wasn’t wasting any novelty mugs on this intruder but I was starting to feel sorry for her. My feelings were annoying me.

She drank slowly. I leaned against the wall cradling my own mug, I still didn’t trust her enough to release the trap. “Start talking or I’m calling the Magical Liaison Office. I think they’d be very interested in one of the cultists who awakened that dragon under the castle.”

Espretha shuddered, “It was awful wasn’t it? I mean I had no idea it would be like that. He said it was a great honour…that we would be serving the true rulers of the world but…we were just food.”

I had not been expecting that. I took a sip of tea so I didn’t have to respond. She seemed like she wanted to talk though, “I managed to get out of there, only just, but still…I tried to call him but he wouldn’t even talk to me, and I couldn’t find him without the pendant. I lost everything. Even my magic has changed. I’ve already handed myself in to the Magical Liaison Office. I’ve been ‘helping them with enquiries’,” somehow she managed to do an air quote with one hand without spilling her drink.

“But, why are you in my bedroom?” I still couldn’t figure that out.

She looked at me as if weighing me up, then looked away, "I thought he might have given you the pendant."

I just blinked at her.

She sighed, exasperated at my slowness, "The oak leaf pendant, I thought Lorandir might have given it to you."

"Oh," I had finally caught up, "erm, well he didn't. Why didn't you just ask?"

She shrugged, "It seemed easier to look for it, besides, I didn't think you'd want to talk to me...and he definitely doesn't"

I rubbed my eyes, she was probably right, but I wasn't particularly happy with the situation now.

"Why did you think he'd give it to me?" I tried to remember back to earlier in the year when Lorandir had seen me with the pendant in the Goat, "I thought it was a friendship charm between you two."

She gave me a look like I was being an idiot but didn't say anything, using my trick of taking a drink of tea. I started to blush without really knowing why.

Finally, she broke the silence, "So, are you going to let me go?"

I narrowed my eyes, picked up my axe, just in case, and thought about the trap I had set. I focused hard, willing it to release her. With a slight gasp, she pulled her hand free.

She gave me a smile then launched herself at me, a blade in her hand appearing from somewhere. I staggered back and brought Bane up to block her. I managed a clumsy parry just in time. She twisted and hit the back of my hand with the hilt of her dagger. I cried out and dropped my axe. I fell to the floor to try to get it back. She stamped her leather boot on my hand. I tried to push her off. She knelt down, keeping one foot on my hand and put her blade to my neck.

"Told you you were holding it wrong!" Abruptly she stood and offered me a hand up. I took it weakly. What the dzrak was that?

"I can teach you to fight better if you like," she shrugged, "the other cultists have got your name from that newspaper article. You might want to learn how to defend yourself."

That bloody newspaper article was the bane of my life.

Other Books in the Series

Thank you for reading book two in the Rise of Dragons series. If you enjoyed this book, you can get a free prequel to the series by joining my mailing list at www.gemmaclatworthy.com.

As an independent author, your reviews help me decide which series to keep going so please do leave one for Solstice of Dragons and if you enjoyed this book, try Equinox Betrayal, book three in the Rise of Dragons series.

Books in the Rise of Dragons series:

Awakening

Solstice of Dragons

Equinox Betrayal

About the Author

Gemma started writing during the 2020 lockdown and loves fantasy fiction and dragons in particular. She lives in Wiltshire with her family and two cats and also enjoys crafts of all kinds and playing board games. Join the conversation at Gemma's book wyrms readers' group on Facebook.

She also writes children's books. You can find out more on her website www.gemmaclatworthy.com or follow her on Instagram (www.instagram.com/gemmaclatworthy) or Facebook (www.facebook.com/gemmaclatworthy).

www.ingramcontent.com/pod-product-compliance
Ingram Content Group UK Ltd.
Pitfield, Milton Keynes, MK11 3LW, UK
UKHW040007200726
13854UKWH00001B/85

9 781915 516022